Fenian Brotherhood Congress

Proceedings of the Second National Congress of the Fenian Brotherhood

held in Cincinnati, Ohio, January, 1865

Fenian Brotherhood Congress

Proceedings of the Second National Congress of the Fenian Brotherhood
held in Cincinnati, Ohio, January, 1865

ISBN/EAN: 9783337381684

Printed in Europe, USA, Canada, Australia, Japan

Cover: Foto ©Andreas Hilbeck / pixelio.de

More available books at **www.hansebooks.com**

PROCEEDINGS

OF THE

Second National Congress

OF THE

Fenian Brotherhood,

HELD IN CINCINNATI, OHIO,

JANUARY, 1865.

"The patient dint and powder shock,
Can blast an empire like a rock."
Thomas Davis.

PHILADELPHIA:
JAMES GIBBONS, PRINTER, 333 CHESTNUT STREET.
1865.

Elective Officers.

The following Minutes, Resolutions, Addresses and By-Laws have been submitted to me and are hereby approved as the Official Report of the SECOND CONGRESS of the Fenian Brotherhood.

Signed,   JOHN O'MAHONY,

H. C. F. B.

PRELIMINARY MEETING.

The Centres and Delegates of the Fenian Brotherhood, summoned by the order of the Head Centre, and Central Council, to meet in Convention at Cincinnati, Ohio, Tuesday, January 17, 1865, at 10 o'clock, A. M., assembled at that hour in preliminary meeting, in Metropolitan Hall. The Head Centre, calling the meeting to order, made the following address:

FELLOW-CITIZENS, CENTRES AND DELEGATES OF THE FENIAN BROTHERHOOD: Before the regular opening of your second annual Congress, for which you are assembled in this hall, I deem it my duty to address you a few preliminary remarks of general interest to yourselves and the Irish and American public The proceedings of Congress will, for obvious reasons, be held with closed doors; matters will have to be discussed here, that if published could not fail to compromise parties who are co-operating with us in another place, and measures will have to be proposed, the premature disclosure of which might give "aid and comfort" to our enemies, inasmuch as the knowledge thus gained of our plans and intentions, would enable those enemies to baffle and circumvent them. We have powerful and wily antagonists to contend against. We can do it only by using the utmost caution and circumspection in our words and actions—by being, if possible, as wily as they. Hence the necessity of withholding from all who do not belong to the Fenian organization many subjects upon which you are assembled here to deliberate. The secret agents and spies of Great Britain and the other enemies of human liberty with whom, unfortunately, this country abounds, may seize upon this as an occasion for renewing against the Fenian Brotherhood the oft refuted accusation of being a Secret Society. But a just public will not be led astray by their assertions.

Our fellow-citizens will not forget that this Brotherhood is virtually at war with the Oligarchy of Great Britain, and that while there is no Fenian army as yet *openly* in the field—such an army nevertheless actually exists, preparing and disciplining itself for freedom's battle, ambushed in the midst of its enemies, watching steadily its opportunity and biding its time. The requirements of our military position will then be a sufficient and satisfactory apology to all but the opponents of our cause for a certain degree of reticence upon our part. The Fenian Congress acts the part of a national assembly of an Irish Republic. Our organized friends in Ireland constitute its army. To divulge the position and intended movements of an army would be to defeat it. It were indeed more conducive to success, if no publicity whatever were given to the existence of our organization, until all our preparations for an uprising of the Irish people were completed. I have myself no objection to *absolute secrecy* in revolutionary associations, provided their objects be just, and their mode of attaining them be pure and honest. But such secrecy would militate against the extension of the Fenian Brotherhood, and prevent it from gaining an amount of popular support sufficient for successful operations. Hence, for the satisfaction of our friends who are not yet enrolled amongst us, I feel compelled on this occasion, to give some information respecting it.

Few men in America are still ignorant of the nature and objects of this organization—those that are to can gain full knowledge thereof in the published acts of our first Congress, held in Chicago in the month of November, 1863. To those acts I refer them, and pass to matters of fresher interest.

CHICAGO CONGRESS—FENIAN GAIN IN 1864.

Previous to our Congress in 1863, the Fenian Brotherhood was but little understood outside its own members. Its representatives had never been summoned together for the purpose of drawing up and adopting such a fixed Constitution, and such rules for its general government, as would have been worthy of an association composed principally of the citizens of a free republic. It had more the nature of a military organization than a civic and self-governing body. This did very well in its infancy; perhaps it was then indispensable. But when it had grown in numbers, intelligence and power, its many disadvantages made themselves felt. The nature of these disadvantages it is needless to dwell upon. They were such as to force upon me the conviction that the organization should be reconstituted after the model of the free institutions of this country—in a word, that the Fenians should make their own laws, elect and control their own officers as is meet that freemen should. Some thousands of our most ardent and best working members had also rushed to the defense of the Union from all our circles.

Many whole circles had entered the American army in a body, like the once flourishing one at Milford, Mass., under its gallant Centre, Peard. In fine, no less than fifty of our branches had become extinct or dormant, and the remainder had lost considerably in ardor and efficiency, through the absence of their choicest spirits in the field. In the West, we had moreover sustained a most irreparable loss in the death of the Rev. Edward O'Flaherty, the devoted pastor of Crawfordsville. Even Indiana, which had been the banner State of the Fenians while he lived. seemed paralyzed when he was no more. It was high time for the Fenians to take counsel together and devise means for the reparation of their losses. , Meanwhile, our brothers in Ireland were crying out for help and sympathy. At the Chicago Congress 63 circles were represented, with a constituency of about 15,000 men, half of whom, at least, were in the armies of the Union, and of the others many were apathetic. As the first result of that Congress, the platform we declared thereat, the Constitution and laws we enacted, have placed us ever since upon a vantage ground that has proved impregnable to every assailant.

The practice of self-government, and the consciousness of the right of supervision over the conduct of its Executive has diffused new vitality and energy throughout every branch of our body politic. At the time when the Congress at Chicago was called the existence of the Fenian Brotherhood in this country mainly depended upon the life of one or two men, and its judicious and successful working depend upon their good sense, talent, honesty and steadfastness. It is no longer dependent for these upon any small number of individuals. It can now change its whole official corps, if found wanting, and yet continue a powerful organization. Is there any true-hearted, thinking Fenian who can regret this? Though there is as yet no legal charter for its incorporation, there are nevertheless as good guarantees for its proper management, as for that of any chartered corporation in this country. There are even better, for its officers can be dismissed whenever they displease their constituencies.

In consequence of the vital energy derived from the Chicago Congress, instead of 63 branches—most of them apathetic, which were there represented, I see around me to-day the Centres, Delegates and proxies of somewhere about 300. making an increase of about 237 circles, most, if not all of them full of life and hope. The increase in our financial receipts has been in proportion to our increased extension. I can safely say that it has exceeded the sum of our receipts during the seven years that have elapsed since the Fenian Brotherhood was first established. In addition to this, the Fenians are undeniably and unmistakably dreaded by the cruel oppressors of Ireland, who auspiciously for our hopes, have also proved themselves to be skulking. ungenerous enemies of America in these days of her most bitter trials. Thus

England has earned the hatred of every true American patriot, as she had long since gained that of every true Irishman. It is no idle boast to say that the English Government has been influenced in no small degree by the action of the Fenians here and at home, in abstaining thus long from openly aiding in the dismemberment of our Union.

Thus, perhaps fortunately for our cause, while working for the liberation of Ireland, we are also serving the best interests of America. Would that we but got as much aid and countenance from the ruling powers in this country as the enemies of the Union are getting from the ruling classes of England. Had we but a few blockade runners at our command we would soon set Great Britain in a blaze of revolution. But the Americans are biding their time; their domestic enemies have given them enough of fighting for the past three or four years. As these must, to all appearances, be vanquished ere long, there will be soon leisure for chastising all the foreign foes of the United States, and more especially perfidious England. The Fenians in the meantime must strive with all their energies to have their preparations so made that our country's tyrant shall not get off with merely a sound whipping. Her tyrannous rule must be utterly destroyed.

We must not indeed rest our hopes altogether upon this or upon any other contingency beyond our actual control. Irishmen alone are fully able to win the freedom of Ireland, if all of them that love her and hate English domination, were working in unison with the Fenian Brotherhood. Let us then place our strongest hope in ourselves alone. All else must be counted as unexpected gain. Our victory would indeed be cheap if the United States were to declare war against the British.

As I said before, the result of our first Congress has been to extend our organization nearly five-fold, and to place it upon so firm a basis that our most malignant enemies cannot destroy it, or even shake it. It has grown in power and public estimation in proportion to the violence of their attacks.

FENIAN LOSSES IN 1864.

Notwithstanding these our great gains, you must not suppose that 1864 has passed over the F. B. without some serious losses and bitter sorrows. The gallant General Michael Corcoran, one of the principal founders of the organization, and one of its most tried and steadfast members to his last hour, has been called away from us to a better world, with his heart's hope unfulfilled. General Corcoran, one of the truest of Irishmen, and of the most loyal of American patriots that has appeared in our day. In him the Brotherhood has lost a most influential member of its Supreme Central Council—prudent, noble, brave and steadfast. In him I, myself, as your chief officer, lost the right arm of my executive corps; as a man, I lost my dearest and most valued friend. We have been deprived by death of many other distinguished officers also; but the Brotherhood will miss none of them more, as effective workers, than Captain Francis Welpley, of the 69th N. Y., Corcoran Legion; Captain James M. Fitzgerald, of the 10th Ohio; Captain O'Shea, N.Y. V., and Major Dufficy, 35th Ind. The circle of the Potomac has been sorely cut up; but a small remnant of its members have escaped the soldier's death. The circle of the Nansemond has been all but annihilated. The circle of the Rappahannock is no more in existence. Having lost heavily in officers and men in the march upon Richmond, it became dispersed when the brave 9th Massachusetts had completed its term of service. But though we lament, we must pride ourselves upon losses like these. Our brothers have died for the Republic.

A vast number of Fenians have fallen in the Army of the Potomac during the last year's campaign. The losses there in officers alone were fearful. Before Richmond it has got to be considered unlucky to be a Fenian. The Fenians make it a point of honor to be ever in the thickest of the fight; hence the very great havoc made amongst them. All honor to the memory of our brave and loyal dead! May America remember them some day with gratitude, and aid us, their brother Fenians, in accomplishing the work which was ever uppermost in their hearts.

OBSTACLES TO THE F. B.

The principal opposition encountered by the Brotherhood during the past year came from certain Catholic clergymen; however, they do not seem to have done us much material injury, considering the great progress we have made in so short a time. We ought, perhaps, even to thank these Reverend opponents for the publicity they gave to our association. It has led many good men to read the acts of the Chicago Congress for themselves, to examine into our objects and Constitution, and to inquire what manner of men we are like.

The result has generally been in our favor. Unjust accusations and unfounded vituperation have often an effect contrary to that intended by their originators. So it has proved in our case. We are at last proof against any amount of clerical abuse, provided we do nothing to deserve it

THE LATE CANADIAN SCARE.

I must here refer to the late terror caused in Canada by the fear of our organization. It proves some useful facts—the dread the provincialists have of us, our power over them, and the extensive spread of our doctrines and work: otherwise it counts for nothing. The Canadian loyalists have made fools of themselves. They have shown how far behind the intellectual progress of the present age they are. They are still as stupid and bigoted as when the Pope and the Pretender were the great bug-bears of loyal Britishers. Let them set their hearts at ease with regard to the Fenian Circles of the Canadas. These are not organized for the purpose of making a revolution in those provinces. Their object has relation to Ireland *alone*. The Canadian Fenians will, however, defend themselves if outraged, and their brothers here will lend them a helping hand if they need it. Let the Loyalists and Orange men keep themselves quiet toward our brothers, and we will let them worship their antiquated idols in peace—save and except we be ordered by our own government to cross the borders in hostile guise. Let them, then, give no more aid and comfort to the enemies of the United States, no more shelter and support to the robbers of our citizens on their frontiers, and let them keep their hands off our brothers in their midst, If they act thus, we promise to do them no bodily harm, unless, as just said, in case of war between their mistress and our adopted country. Think of their being frightened by the Fenians into calling for 100,000 volunteers to meet an attack from us while we were not even thinking of them!

ORGANIZATIONS IN IRELAND.

We have heard of Fenians in Ireland; also Fenian principles, Fenian aspirations and Fenian work are undeniably widely spread there, and also Fenian men. It is there they have the most right to be. But this American institution called the Fenian Brotherhood does not exist there as an organized body. By this assertion I do not mean to say that no organized body of revolutionists exists on the Irish soil at present, co-operating with this Brotherhood, and to a great extent, sustained and encouraged by it. All our labors up to this would have been in vain had we not such an organization working in unison with us, for it is in Ireland that organization is most needed There English tyranny must receive the death blow. Now that we have more trained soldiers and competent officers of our own race and our own feelings in America than we can ever require, there would be no need of organizing our countrymen here were it not that it is indispensible to the attainment of our object at home that we should aid in discipliuing and arming the men who are desirous of striking for liberty there. What need is there of enrolling men here in the F. B. for the invasion of Ireland? If all other things needed for such an expedition were provided, we would have but to beat the drum through the streets of New York, and that city alone would furnish a sufficient number of volunteers for it in twenty-four hours. There is no necessity in banding Irishmen together in this country for that purpose. It is for the purpose of organizing our kinsfolks at home that the Fenian Brotherhord is in existence. That is our most certain means of liberating our fatherland. We are firmly convinced that no enslaved people ever won liberty without pre-organization; and we are determined that Ireland shall be pre-organized.

The envoy of your Central Council, who has just returned from his tour through Ireland, will report to you, when in regular session, how far our labors there have been successful. The name under which our Irish allies are enrolled is to be found in one of the unpublished resolutions of our first Congress, which shall be read to you for your confirmation. They do their work quietly, as the exigency of their position demands, and seldom become known to any but their associates. Their system differs greatly from ours, and they are under different executive control. They are, I need not tell you, deemed illegal by English law,

There are also other political organizations in Ireland. At the head of one of them are two very worthy Irish gentlemen, Mr. John Martin and the O'Donoghue. This is a legal and constitutional body, according to the British acceptation of the words. Its avowed object is to relieve the woes of Ireland by publishing them to foreign nations and by open agitation. It has few adherents among the people who have already suffered too many losses by agitation, and who want no more of it. Its leaders appeal to French and other European sympathy, but overlook the immense power that might be brought to bear against the desolators of their country by appealing to this side of the Atlantic, and by co-operating with the Fenians. They seem to dread military organization, or else to despair of its possibility. The French know how they expelled their own tyrants, and will tell them to do likewise— namely, to organize steadily and silently, after a military manner. These gentlemen ignore Fenianism, and Fenianism ignores them. For my part, however, I would gladly unite with them in working out Ireland's freedom if they would give up public agitation, and commence to organize an Irish army of deliverance in Ireland, after a business-like, revolutionary fashion. The other organization promises to be nothing more than a workshop for place-hunters of the Sadlier-Keogh style. The venerable and patriotic Archbishop McHale has, it is to be devoutly hoped, crushed it in its infancy by his late letter. I was sorry to find Mr. John B. Dillon, the Irish Revolutionist of '48, lending his name to it.

Such are the political organizations existing at present in Ireland. There is no national vitality in the land outside the ranks of our own allies and brothers of whom you shall hear by and by. Yet Ireland is perishing from exhaustion; her sons are rushing in thousands from her shores. If she be saved at all she must be saved by the Fenians and their allies—and even they must be quick in their movements, or they shall soon have no country to save.

RESPONSIBILITY OF THE CONGRESS.

I will now remind you of the great responsibility that devolves upon you on the present occasion. The successes of the Fenian cause—the Freedom of Ireland and the preservation of her race—depend upon the wisdom, devotion and pure patriotism that shall guide your acts and deliberations. The des-

troyers of our race will have their agencies at work amongst you, if gold can
effect it. I speak even no , as if I were in the presence of those destroyers
and their agents. Their spies may be and probably are in this hall. However, I trust that our Congressional arrangements will be such as to defeat
their evil intentions. We must avoid saying more than is absolutely necessary
of our allies in Ireland. Their names should never be mentioned except in
select committees, where they cannot be avoided. We are ourselves beyond
the reach of British malignity, as far as regards our persons and property.
It is only by sowing discord in our midst that our enemies can defeat us. Let
us then, with common accord, crush the slightest symptoms of that fell bane
of Ireland wherever it appears. The man who gives way to petty jealousies
or angry vituperations in our midst should be treated as an agent of England,
for, however, free from corrupt motives, he performs the work that is now
most useful to her. In no other way can she reach us. There must, of course,
be freedom of opinion and of suffrage ; but when a question is once decided
by vote the will of the majority must be the universal law of all. Thus shall
the God of your sires bless your councils and crown your deliberations with
success, and thus shall He enable you to defeat the machinations of all your
foes.

THE FINANCES—CONDUCT OF OFFICERS—ELECTIONS.

The financial receipts and expenditures of the past year will be fairly laid
before you, and submitted to you by your Central Treasurer, for your approval
or condemnation. The official conduct of your President, or Head Centre, of
your Supreme Central Council, of your Central Treasurers and State Centres,
will have to be decided upon by you also. They will be one and all on their
trial before you in this hall. You will have to either re-elect them or elect
others in their places.

You will, moreover, have to deliberate upon the experience of the past
year ; to reconsider whatever you deem faulty in our organization, and to
adopt measures to meet the requirements of the present and future. If you
act wisely, firmly and justly, this will be the beginning of a new era in the
Fenian organization. Above all things, in all considerations and debates,
cultivate conciliation, forbearance and fraternal harmony. Your love of
Ireland is now about to be measured by your love of one another.

In a few hours I will be myself a private member of your body. My official
career since I became the object of your choice will be before you. Of it I
shall say nothing calculated to influence your judgment in my favor or against
me. I have done my best according to the best of my own judgment, for the
safety and extension of the organization. If I have failed in any particular
to have always acted for its best interests, my judgment, not my will, was at
fault. I do not court re-election. Should you choose another person as your
Head Centre for 1865, I shall support him with whatever influence I may
possess, while ever he acts up to your principles and laws, and while he en-
forces them.

You will immediately proceed to propose the appointment of three preliminary committees. A Committee on credentials first. The duty devolving
upon this committee is exceedingly grave. It will have to examine accurately
the credentials of every applicant for admission, so as to prevent British spies
from coming in here during our session, and not only British, but the spies of
any other enemy. We had British spies and secret agents in Chicago, at our
first Congress, though then weak compared with our present strength. We
are now a real power in the community, consequently there will be a host of
these spies after and around us wherever we go for the next three or four
days. The second Committee is one on permanent officers ; and the third
one on regulations for the Congress. Those committees when appointed, must
come before the Central Council for instructions before proceeding to business.

The address being concluded,

H. O'C. McCarthy moved that Colonel W. G. Halpin, of Cincinnati, act as Secretary *pro tem.* Seconded and carried unanimously.

J. W. Fitzgerald, of Ohio, moved that there be three Committees appointed —namely, Committee on Credentials, Committee on Permanent Officers, and Committee on Rules and Regulations for the Convention; which motion being seconded, was carried unanimously, and the Committees were appointed by the Chairman as follows:

P. W. DUNNE, Ills., THOS. B. HENNESSEY, Mass., P. BANNON, Ky., J. J. ROGERS, N. Y W. MORAN, Mo.,	Committee on Credentials.
JAMES GIBBONS, Penna., M. SCANLIN, Ills., J. MANNING, Ohio., L. VERDON, Mich., J. C. O'BRIEN, N. Y.,	Committee on Permanent Officers.
J. W. FITZGERALD, Ohio., THOMAS HAIRE, Ills., W. J. HYNES, N. E., DANIEL DONOVAN, Mass., CORNELIUS MURPHY, Penna.,	Committee on Rules and Regulations.

On motion of P. Cooney, of N. Y., the Preliminary Meeting then adjourned to 3 o'clock, P. M., in order to afford the respective committees an opportunity to prepare their reports.

Afternoon Session.

The Congress was called to order by the H. C. F. B. at 3½ o'clock.

The Chair appointed the following gentlemen a Committee to assign seats to the different delegations.

M. SCANLAN Ills., JAMES LACKEY, D. C., JOHN HOWLEY, Ills.,	Committee on Assigned Seats.

The Committee on Credentials not being prepared to report or act, and it being consequently impossible to determine with accuracy who were entitled to seats in organized session, the Congress on motion adjourned over until 9 o'clock, A. M., Wednesday the 18th inst.

First Organized Session.

Wednesday, January 18, 1865.—Pursuant to adjournment, the Congress was called to order at 9 o'clock, A. M. by the H. C. F. B.

P. W. Dunne, Ills., Chairman of Committee on Credentials presented the report of that Committee, which upon motion was adopted.

Committee on Permanent Officers made the following report which was adopted.

President, JOHN O'MAHONY.

Vice Presidents,
- W. MORAN, Mo.
- P. W. DUNNE, Ills.
- Capt. MICHAEL BAILEY, N. Y.
- WM. GRIFFIN, Ind.
- THOMAS DOODY, Mass.
- P. BANNON, Ky.

Secretaries,
- Colonel W. G. HALPIN, Department Cumberland.
- J. AUSTEN STEWART, Ind.
- THOMAS HURLEY, N. Y.
- WILLIAM DELANY, Conn.
- BARTHOLOMEW HIGGINS, N. Y.

On motion the resignations of J. A. Stewart and B. Higgins were accepted and the Chair appointed F. J. Grant, Ind., and W. J. Hynes, N. E. to fill the vacancies.

The Committee on Rules and Regulations for the government of the Congress, reported the following which were adopted.

RULES AND REGULATIONS.

1st. All credentials shall be submitted to the Committee on Credentials.

2d. All motions shall upon call of two delegates be submitted in writing.

3d. All speakers shall speak to the *point* under debate. No one shall be allowed to speak more than once, or more than fifteen minutes on the same subject, except in explanation, such explanation to occupy no more than five minutes.

4th. No personalities shall be allowed.

5th. Strict silence shall be observed when the President's gavel falls.

6th. The President shall decide all questions before the Congress.

7th. The sessions of the convention shall be held as follows. Morning session from 9 A. M. to 1 P. M. ; Afternoon session from 2 P. M. to 6 P. M.

8th. The code of regulations set down in Jefferson's Manual shall, in all else, govern the Congress.

The Secretary read the minutes of the preceding session which upon motion were adopted.

The President of the Congress, John O'Mahony, then delivered the following address.

* * * * * * *

THE WORK AT HOME.

The Fenian Brotherhood is founded upon the conviction that a military organization at home is absolutely essential to the liberation of Ireland. The Irish Revolutionary Brotherhood, with which we are in alliance and the sustainment of which is one of our chief objects, is the only association in our native country which is likely to effect its disenthralment. It is, in my opinion, the only one that can be formed in our day. *If it be allowed to go down for want of sufficient subsidies, the Fenian Brotherhood will have existed in vain, and Ireland's hope of freedom will be destroyed for the present generation.* Think earnestly and honestly upon this fact and allow no paltry considerations to distract your minds from its thorough comprehension. Our object is as grand as it is just and holy. The magnitude of the work before us is immense. It is nothing less than the disruption of one of the most mighty empires of the world, and the resurrection of a nationality that has lain prostrate for three hundred years. It is true, that we are more favorably located for working out our designs than was ever any enslaved nationality before us, it is true, that the tyrant of Ireland is more at the mercy of the Irish people to-day, than was ever the tyrant of any suffering nationality. We have the power within reach to destroy the domination of that tyrant. But to do so effectively we must learn how to discipline and unite the scattered elements of that power and direct its combined force against our country's foe. Our countrymen, and all who love Ireland, must be organized in these United States. Here a never-failing base of supplies must be created and secured, the Irishmen of the British colonies aiding in the work. Our Brothers in Ireland and Great Britain must be thoroughly organized for insurrection and their organization must be liberally subsidized as well as armed and supplied with military officers by the Fenian Brotherhood.

*　　*　　*　　*　　*　　*　　*

*　　*　　*　　*　　*　　*　　*

It is this Brotherhood that is to furnish the supplies and munitions of war while our friends at home furnish the soldiers to use them. Were funds available for that purpose, I would recommend the transmission of as large sums as possible to Europe for the purchase of arms, &c.

MILITARY ORGANIZATION IN AMERICA.

It is evident that our brothers in Ireland need military leaders and competent line officers to act under them. Hence I recommend the immediate formation of a military branch of the Fenian Brotherhood. Over this a special officer should be appointed, subject to the orders of your President or Head Centre. The said officer and his command should hold themselves constantly in readiness to go to Ireland.

As the probabilities of war between the United States and England are every day becoming more evident, and as the chances of an armed expedition to Ireland are growing greater, I strongly recommend the formation of a military corps by the younger members of the Fenian Brotherhood in all cities and towns of the Union. New York should have its Fenian Brigade, Philadelphia, Cincinnati, Boston, Chicago, their Fenian Regiments. All these should hold themselves in constant readiness either to sail at once for Europe or to march into the British Provinces at the command of the United States authorities. In case of a war, such as I mention, the chances of successful invasion would be greatly increased by our being found ready to march in a few hours after its proclamation became known. A fund should be set apart, and lodged in safe custody, in New York, subject to the orders of the Central Council, for the purpose of sending skilful military men to Ireland in sufficient numbers previous to any uprising of her people; or, should such be found practicable, for fitting out an armed expedition.

A PROVISIONAL GOVERNMENT.

I moreover suggest to you the propriety of authorizing your incoming officers, after due consideration of the subject, to form a Provisional Government. You are now in a position, in point of numbers and respectability, to take this course. It will be your own fault if you do not select from amongst you those who are both fully competent for the duty and worthy of any trust you may repose in them.

EXTENSION OF THE FENIAN BROTHERHOOD.

For the past six months our organization in America has been worked to the utmost extent that its financial resources would bear. No man, however impatient, can say that it has not been urged ahead most energetically. Still it requires time to make the circles recently founded by our central organizers financially profitable to the organization. As you will see by the reports about to be presented to you those circles are as yet far from clearing the cost of their formation. They are, however, a source of great moral strength to us, and will, I trust, be financially profitable ere long. I request all that complain of the former slowness of our progress to take these facts into their most serious consideration.

CONSTITUTION AND BY-LAWS.

The members of your Committee on Constitution and By-Laws should be selected from amongst the ablest and most earnest men in your Congress. Their duty is a most important one. There should also be men of adequate literary attainments among them, Some knowledge of legal forms would be most desirable, so as to remedy all ambiguity in phraseology. In your By-Laws especially, the complete independence of the Fenian Brotherhood of all other organizations should be unmistakably enunciated. Your officers should be declared accountable to yourselves alone. Many future difficulties and embarrassments will be avoided by precision on this point.

THE CENTRAL COUNCIL.

I suggest that the Central Council, to be nominated at this Congress, be empowered to increase its number to ten, and that it should have power to elect an officer to preside over it, and that he be styled President of the Central Council. Five, with this officer, should constitute a quorum. The increase in number is for the purpose of embracing within it as many elements of Irish nationhood as possible, and to enable it to meet more frequently than heretofore. It should be the prerogative of the Central Council to call either a convention of State Centres or a general convention, and thereat impeach and depose the Head Centre, should he be found unworthy of his position. It should also be empowered to receive the Head Centre's resignation, and nominate a Provisional Head Centre to fill the vacancy till the next ensuing meeting of your Congress. The President of the Central Council should be next in rank and authority to the Head Centre, and should represent him when absent from the Headquarters of the Brotherhood. He should also have the supervision of all financial receipts and expenditures, but should order no disbursements without the sanction of the Head Centre, unless by special vote of the Central Council.

ELECTION OF HEAD CENTRE AND STATE CENTRES.

One of the last, and not the least important duties you will have to perform, will be the election of your Head Centre for 1865. Now is your time to fix upon a man worthy of that trust. Look around you carefully, and be fully alive to the gravity of the duty you will have so soon to perform. The object of your choice will morally be invested with the highest honor that can be conferred upon him by his fellow-citizens. The duties to be discharged by him are as grave as those of the President, or first officer, of an independent nationality. From small beginnings, the Fenian Brotherhood h s become a great power. No men, or class of men on earth can any more look down upon an organization represented by such an assemblage as I see in this hall, from all parts of America. We have conquered the respect of even our enemies. For myself, I am satisfied with what I have performed thus far in the service of the Fenian Brotherhood. In its infancy, and in the perils of its slow and painful growth, I watched and tended it with anxious care. It is now arrived at vigorous maturity, and it can henceforth take care of itself. My guardianship ends here. I commit it to its own direction and control.

The observations I have made in reference to the selection of your future Head Centre are also applicable to the selection of State Centres. In all cases discard the promptings of faction and favoritism. In every instance strive to choose men who are the most capable and trustworthy.

Upon the conclusion of this address, the regular business was entered upon.

On motion. the Secretary was directed to condense the minutes of each session for publication in the newspapers.

On motion, the following report of the organizers in relation to the number and condition of circles was read and approved :

Report of Circles.
Massachusetts.

No.	NAMES OF CIRCLES.	When last reported.	In bad standing.
1	Haverhill	Jan. 6, '65	
2	North Abington	Oct. 28, '64	
3	Spencer	Dec. 1, "	
4	Gardiner	Dec. 21, "	
5	East Boston	Dec. 28, "	
6	South Boston	Nov. 30, "	
7	Somerville	Dec. 28, "	
8	Worcester	" 31, "	
9	Stoneham	" — "	
10	Charlestown	Nov. 28, "	
11	Brighton	" 25, "	
12	Winchenden	Dec. 28, "	
13	Haydenville	Jan. 4, '65	
14	Boston	Dec. 31, '64	
15	Greenfield	" — "	
16	Lawrence	" 27, "	
17	Holyoke	" 27, "	
18	Hopkinton	" 31, "	
19	West Cambridge	June 13, "	West Cambridge
20	Natick	Dec. 6, "	
21	Dedham	" 31, "	
22	Lowell	Nov. 28, "	
23	Gilbertsville	Dec. 29, "	
24	Chicoppee	" 29, "	
25	Taunton	May 29, "	Taunton
26	Chelsea	Dec. 29, "	
27	South Reading	Nov. 26, "	
28	Springfield	Dec. 29, "	
29	Brookline	Nov. 5, "	
30	Lynn		
31	Point Lookout, Md.	Nov. 28, '64	
32	Salem		
33	Woburn		
34	Roxbury		
35	South End, MacMannus S. C. Boston		
36	Emmett Sub-Circle		
37	Milford		
38	Cherry Valley		

Total in good standing—36 Circles
"   "   bad   "   2

Rhode Island.

No.	NAMES OF CIRCLES.	When last reported.	
1	Greenville	Jan. 6, '65	
2	Woonsocket	Dec. 29, '64	
3	Providence	Nov. 26, "	
4	Peace Dale	Dec. 22, "	
5	Valley Falls	Jan. 4, '65	

Total in good standing—5 Circles

Maine.

1	Vinal Haven		

Connecticut.

No.	NAMES OF CIRCLES.	When last reported.	In bad standing.
1	Hartford - - -	Sept. 27, '64	
2	Birmingham - - -	June 18, '64	Birmingham
3	New Haven - - -		
4	Waterbury - - -	Organ. Jan. 4,	
5	West Meridian - -	" Jan. 3, '65	
6	Bridgeport - - -	" " 7, '65	
	Total in good standing—5 Circles		
	" " bad " 1 "		

New Hampshire.

No.	NAMES OF CIRCLES.	When last reported.	In bad standing.
1	Wilton - - -	Dec. 19, '64	
2	Nashua - - -	" 31, "	
3	Manchester . - -	Jan. 4, '65	
4	Claremont - - -	recent formt'n	
5	Keene - - -	"	
6	Concord - - -	"	
7	Exeter - - -	"	
	Total in good standing—7 Circles		

Vermont.

No.	NAMES OF CIRCLES.	When last reported.	In bad standing.
1	Windsor - - -	Recently form	
2	Brattleboro' - -	"	
3	Rutland - - -	"	
4	Burlington - -	"	
	Total in good standing—4 Circles		

District of Manhattan—City of New York.

No.	NAMES OF CIRCLES.	When last reported.	In bad standing.
1	Hamilton Rowan Club - -		
2	Phœnix Zouaves - -		
3	Wolfe Tone - - -		
4	Wolfe Tone Cadets - -		
5	Doheny Circle - . -		
6	Fontenoy Cadets - ,		
7	Lavelle - - -		
8	Benburb - - -		
9	Stapleton, Staten Island - -		
10	Roseville " - -		
11	Factoryville " - -		
12	Tara Circle Brooklyn - -		
13	Yonkers - . - -		
14	Spuyten Duyvill - -		
15	Mac Manus - - -		
16	Davis - - -		
17	O'Mahony - - -		
18	Sarsfield - - -		
19	McHale - - -		
20	Emmett. Williamsburg -		
	Total in good standing—20 Circles		

New York.

No.	NAMES OF CIRCLES.	When last reported.	In bad standing.
1	Troy	Dec. 29, '64	
2	West Troy	Jan. 3, '65	
3	Waterford	Dec. 23, '64	
4	Buffalo	large remit.	
5	Oswego	Nov. 9, '64	
6	Saratoga Springs	Nov. 28, "	
7	Cohoes	" 28 "	
8	Davis Circle, Troy	Dec. 29, "	
9	Albany	Jan. 4, '65	
10	Brighton	New	
11	Schenectady		
12	Elmira	Dec. 30, '64	
13	Ilion	New	
14	Herkimer	Dec. 24, '64	
15	Saugerties	Nov. 23, "	
16	Rome		Rome
17	Syracuse	Dec. 21, '64	
18	Auburn	" 29, "	
19	Seneca Falls	" 30, "	
20	Canandagua	New	
21	Brockport	Dec. 27, '64	
22	Malone	" 28, "	
23	Rochester	" 28, "	
24	Watertown	" 27, "	
25	Utica	" 21, "	
26	Dunkirk	" 30, "	
27	Cooperstown	Jan. 3, '65	

Total in good standing—26 Circles
  "   "   bad   "   1   "

New Jersey.

1	Newark	Dec. 23, '64	
2	Jersey City, Emmett	Nov. 14, "	
3	Hudson City	New	

Total in good standing—3 Circles

Pennsylvania.

1	Philadelphia	Dec. 29, '64	
2	Broad Top	Jan. 5, '65	
3	Pittsburgh	Dec. 29, '64	
4	Wilksbarre	June 29, '64	Wilksbarre
5	Carbondale	Feb. 29, '64	
6	St. Clair	April 4, "	St. Clair
7	Pottsville	June 15, "	Pottsville
8	New Philadelphia	Feb. 29, "	New Phila.
9	Altoona	Dec. 22, "	
10	Ashland	New	
11	Meadville	New	
12	Erie	New	
13	Warren	New	
14	Lock Haven	New	
15	Williamsport	New	
16	Danville	New	

Total in good standing—12 Circles
  "   "   bad   "   4   "

Ohio.

No.	NAMES OF CIRCLES.	When last reported.	In bad standing.
1	Cleveland	Nov. 25, '64	
2	*Columbus	Jan. 7, '65	
3	Ironton	June 20, '64	
4	Crestline	Dec. 31, '64	
5	Cincinnati	" 16, "	
6	Dayton	Oct. 28, "	
7	Lancaster	Dec. 30, "	
8	Tennystown	Jan. 3, '65	
9	Hudson	Dec. 2, '64	
10	Toledo	Nov. 20, "	
11	Richmond	Jan. 3, '65	
12	Tiffin		
13	Springfield	New	
14	Urbana	"	
15	Marion	"	
16	Crestline	"	
17	Mansfield	"	
18	Ackson	"	
	Total in good standing—17 Circles		
	" " bad " 1		

*About to remit.

Illinois.

1	Bloomington	Sept. 5, '64	
2	Camp Point	Jan. 4, '65	
3	Mount Sterling	" "	
4	Wilmington	Nov. 30, '64	
5	Galesburg	Dec. 24, "	
6	Galena	Oct. 31, "	
7	Bloomfield	April 30, "	
8	La Salle	Dec. 12, "	
9	Joliet	" 30, "	
10	Seneca	" 29, "	
11	Springfield	Jan. 9, '65	
12	Peoria	" 6, "	
13	Danville	Dec. 28, '64	
14	Alton	Jan. 7, '65	
15	Chicago	Dec. 29, '64	
16	Cairo	" 31, "	
17	Morris	" 29, "	
18	Ottowa	Nov. 7, "	
19	Gillman	June 30, "	
20	Amboy	Dec. 31, "	
21	Quincy	Jan. 3, '65	
22	Lacon		
23	Dixon		
24	Rock Island		
25	Freeport		
	Total in good standing—24 Circles		
	" bad " 1 "		

District of Columbia.

No.	NAMES OF CIRCLES.	When last reported.	In bad standing.
1	Washington - - -	Jan, 5, '65.	

Iowa.

No.	NAMES OF CIRCLES.	When last reported.	In bad standing.
1	Des Moines - - -	July 2, '64.	Des Moines.
2	Davenport - - -	Jan. 6, '65.	
3	McGregor - - -	" 5, "	
4	Walnut Grove - -	July 13, '64.	
5	Lansing - - - -	Nov. 2, "	
6	Burlington - - -	Jan 10, '65.	
7	Keokuk - - - -	" 3, "	
8	Iowa City - - -	Aug. 1, '64.	Iowa City.
9	El Kader - - - -	Dec. 31, "	
10	Ottumwa - - -	New	
11	Dubuque - - - -	"	
12	Rosville - - -	"	
13	Muscatine - - -	"	
14	Wexford - - -	"	
	Total in good standing—12 circles.		
	" " bad " 2		

Wisconsin.

No.	NAMES OF CIRCLES.	When last reported.	In bad standing.
1	Horicon - - - -	Jan. 29,' 64.	Horican.
2	La Crosse - - -	Dec. 28, "	
3	Osh Kosh - - -	" 31, "	
4	Milwaukie - - -		
5	Prairie du Chien - -	New.	
6	Fon du Lac - - -	"	
7	Janesville - - -	"	
8	Madison - - -	"	
9	Racine - - - -	"	
10	Green Bay - - -	"	
	Total in good standing—9 Circles.		
	" " bad " 1 "		

Michigan.

No.	NAMES OF CIRCLES.	When last reported.	In bad standing.
1	Ontonagon - - -		
2	Detroit - - -	Dec. 29, '64.	
3	Rockland - -		
4	Wyandotte - - -		
5	Grand Rapids - -		
6	Ishpenning - - -		
7	Berlin - - -		
	Total in good standing—7 Circles.		
	" " bad " 2		
	Circles mostly report through Detroit.		

Minnesota.

No.	NAMES OF CIRCLES.	When last reported.	In bad standing.
1	St. Paul - - - -	New	
2	Winona - - - -	Dec. 10, '65	
	Total in good standing—2 Circles		

Indiana.

No.	NAMES OF CIRCLES.	When last reported.	In bad standing
1	Indianapolis	Sept. 23, '64	
2	Jeffersonville	Jan. 4, '65	
3	Aurora	" 3, "	
4	Lafayette	Oct. 13, '64	
5	Delphi	Dec. 31, "	
6	Logansport	Jan. 6, '65	
7	La Porte	Dec. 21, '64	
8	Madison	" 10, "	
9	Mitchell	" 31, "	
10	Richmond	" 28, "	
11	New Albany	Jan. 3, 65	
12	Bloomington	Dec. 30, '64	
13	Greencastle	Jan. 4, '65	
14	Beadford	Dec. 31, '64	
15	Terre Haute	Jan. 3, '65	
16	Shelbyville	Dec. 24, '64	
17	Crawfordsville	" 27, "	
18	Valparaiso	" 28, "	
19	Lawrenceburg	Jan 3, '65	
20	Columbus	" 6, "	
21	Michigan City	New	
22	Fort Wayne	"	
23	Edinburgh	"	
	Total in good standing—20 Circles		
	" " bad " 3 "		

Missouri.

No.	NAMES OF CIRCLES.	When last reported.	In bad standing
1	Rolla	June 18, '64	
2	St. Charles	Jan. 7, '65	
3	Hannibal	" 4, "	
4	Brookfield	Sept. 12, '64	
5	St. Louis	New	
	Total in good standing—5 Circles		

Tennessee.

No.	NAMES OF CIRCLES.	When last reported.	In bad standing
1	Nashville	Dec. 4, '64	
2	Clarksville	June 29, "	
3	Memphis	No report.	Memphis
	Total in good standing—2 Circles		
	" bad " 1 "		

Kentucky.

No.	NAMES OF CIRCLES.	When last reported.	In bad standing
1	Louisville	Dec. 12, "	
2	Lexington	Jan. 3, '65	
3	Bowling Green	May 9, '65	Bowling Green
4	Frankfort	New	
	Total in good standing—3 Circles.		
	" bad " 1 "		

Kansas.

No.	NAMES OF CIRCLES.	When last reported.	In bad standing.
1	Lavenworth - - -	Jan. 9, '65	
2	Atchenson - - -	" 3, "	
3	Fort Scott - - -	Dec. 6, '65	
	Total in good standing—3 Circles.		

Oregon, Utah, Nevada and Idaho.

1	Portland, Oregon - -		
2	Camp Douglass, Utah - -		
3	Virginia City, Nevada -		
4	Virginia, Idaho - - -		
	Total in good standing—4 Circles.		

California

1	San Francisco - - -		
2	Sacramento - - -		
3	San Jose - - , - -		
4	Copperopolis - - -		
5	Los Angelos - - -		
6	Fort Ruby - - -		
7	Santa Clara - - - -		
8	Moore's Flat - - -		
9	Eureka South - - -		
10	Presidio - - -		
11	Alkatrer Island - - -		
12	Camp Reynolds - - -		
13	Lawyer's Bar - - -		
	Report through Cavanagh of San Francico.		

U. S. Army and Navy.

1	10th Ohio Circle - -	June 4, '64	10th Ohio
2	15th Michigan - -	April 6, '64	15th Mich.
3	Nansemond—Corcoran Legion -	Oct. 11, "	
4	Potomac Circle - - -	Jan. 8, '65	
5	U. S. Engineers - -	Oct. 20, '64	
6	Potomac Sub-Circle - -	April 26, "	Pot. Sub-Circle
7	U. S. Frigate New Ironsides - -	Dec. 3, '64	
8	" " Huntsville -	Aug. 4, "	
9	Morris Island, S. C. - - -	Jan. 6, '65	
10	U. S. Steamer " Port Royal" -	Dec. 17,'64	
11	" Brooklyn -		
12	Gleason Sub-Circle - -		
	Total in good standing—12 Circles.		
	" bad " 1 "		

British Provinces.

1	Montreal C. E. - - -	Dec. 24, '64	
2	Toronto C. W. - - -	" 9, "	
	Total in good standing—2 Circles.		

Aggregation.

NAMES OF DISTRICTS.	Circles in good standing	Circles in bad standing	Total
Massachusetts	36	2	38
Rhode Island	5		5
Connecticut	5	1	6
New Hampshire	7		7
Vermont	4		4
Maine	1		1
District of Manhattan, New York	19		19
New York	26	1	27
New Jersey	3		3
Pennsylvania	12	4	16
Ohio	17	1	18
Illinois	24	1	25
Indiana	20	3	23
District of Columbia	1		1
Iowa	12	2	14
Wisconsin	9	1	10
Michigan	7	2	9
Minnesota	2		2
Missouri	5		5
Tennessee	2	1	3
Kentucky	3	1	4
Kansas	3		3
Oregon, &c.	4		4
California	13		13
U. S. Army and Navy	7	4	11
British Provinces	2		2
Grand Totals.	247	24	273

Upon motion the financial report of the work of organizers was read and adopted. After which Congress adjourned to re-assemble at 2 o'clock, P. M.

Afternoon Session.

At 2 o'clock, P. M., the President called Congress to order.

On motion an order was directed to be drawn on the Central Treasurer for the amount necessary to liquidate the expenses of the Central Organizers.

P. W. Dunne, Ills., read an additional report of the Committee on Credentials, which, upon motion was adopted.

Philip Coyne, Mo., Central Envoy to Ireland, read a lengthy report of his examination and inspection of revolutionary affairs in Ireland, which was received with rapturous applause and unanimously adopted.

(For obvious reasons this report is for the present withheld from the general public.)

"IRISH PEOPLE" NEWSPAPER.

In connection with the paper—the *Irish People*, it is my firm conviction that the existence of this journal is essential to the spirit and strength of the Irish organization, the good it has already effected is worth its outlay *tenfold*, as you are doubtless aware from the fearless and able manner in which it is conducted. It gives courage and strength to those who are made the subject of denunciations and of petty, malignant tyrany, as it exposes the hostility and character of the *denunciators* regardless of former influence or present standing.

The most strenuous exertions should be made by Irish American patriots, to give this able advocate of Irish liberty a circulation adequate to the talents vigor and honesty, concentrated in its column. The price paid for it is *less* than any other weekly paper in Ireland—in order that it may come within the means of the many poor men belonging to the organization, and as an inducement to others to purchase it, so they may learn and *profit* by its teachings.

THE MASSES—THE PEOPLE.

The spirit of the people—The masses favor and desire—REVOLUTION! it being the ONLY MEANS for righting themselves. There are many in Ireland who keep aloof now, but who would *act* when occasion requires, especially if the Brotherhood in America will give the aid expected of them.

The *masses* in Ireland do not any longer look up to the old political *agitators* except in the light of suspicion as political hacks and place-hunters.

The present political (assumed) leaders in Ireland—those who are most frequently before the people in print are JOHN MARTIN, THE O'DONOGHUE, J. B. DILLON, and a few others of lesser note. The actions of these men tend still towards the old worn-out system of AGITATION. They are now inaugurating, or endeavoring to inaugurate, another phase of this same agitation, but the people have no confidence whatever in the idea that any good for *the country* can be gained by such *empty measures*. The people are therefore perfectly indifferent whether he be an *Archbishop* or a provincial attorney who attempts to institute or promulgate agitation—they know full well that if physical force were necessary in the days when some of these men taught that doctrine, how much more is, it required now when the enemy is using every means of extermination. The prevailing sentiment throughout the country is that these leaders are fully cognizant of the fact, that agitation is a dead letter. These assumed leaders *feeling* the advanced state of Irish Nationality and the spirit of independence with which the masses are rapidly becoming imbued, endeavor to divert them by this LEGAL DECOY into the slavish doctrine that "liberty is not worth the spilling of one drop of blood." These agitators are understood and cannot divert the attention of the *true* men at home from prosecuting the work to which they have solemnly pledged themselves.

THE I. R. B. MODE OF ORGANIZING.

The mode of organization of the I. R. B. seemed to me to be as nearly perfect as possible; it is so arranged as to defy the strongest power or finest subtility to penetrate it.

EXISTING "CLASSES" IN IRELAND.

There are in Ireland three classes—the aristocratic, the middle, and the lower class. The first of these are Anti-Irish, the second are in a great degree practical Anti-nationalists—they would love liberty for their land, but occupying pleasant positions and contemplating with profound awe, "the power of England"—they hesitate to pass into a career of trial, labor, and perhaps oppose, rather than stimulate, any movement in that direction. However, it may safely be said that, in a revolutionary outbreak, when men must of necessity take sides, this class will act boldly and heartily with the revolutionists. The third class—the *people*,—are thoroughly aroused, the existence of the organized body is not only recognized, but its pulsations are felt in every part of the national system. During the past year, and more particularly since the issue of the "IRISH PEOPLE," this spirit has been growing. The tens of thousands available men—men outside the organization, who have been deterred by threats or fears, or by a blind obedience to the dicta of a clergyman, begin to manifest uneasiness when the creed of Fenianism is assailed and in many instances join hands with the banded patriots, in resenting the malicious and frequently dangerous accusations.

On motion the thanks of the Congress were presented to Mr. Coyne, for his able and satisfactory report.

P. Cooney, N. Y. offered the following resolution—"Resolved that the thanks of this Congress be and the same are hereby presented to P. W. Dunne, Esq., of Peoria, Ills., for his munificent donations to the Fenian Brotherhood;" seconded and carried unanimously.

A similar vote of thanks was presented to Wm. Moran, Esq., of St. Louis, Mo.

The Central Treasurer's Report was next read and on motion referred to the Committee on Finance.

Colonel B. F. Mullen, Ind., offered the following resolution—"Resolved that so much of the Head Centre's address as relates to military affairs be referred to a Military Committee, and that the President be empowered to appoint said Committee; seconded and carried."

Being then 6 o'clock the President declared the Congress adjourned until 9 o'clock, Thursday, January 19th, 1865.

Third Day's Session.

THURSDAY, JANUARY 19, 1865.

The Congress was called to order by the President at 9 o'clock, A. M.

On motion of H. O'C. McCarthy, the State Centres were directed to report to the Secretary, the names of such delegates as had not yet been placed on the roll, that they may be entered thereon.

The Roll was then called.

The minutes of the preceeding day were read by the Secretary, and, upon motion, adopted unanimously.

On motion of M. J. O'Reilly, Mich., the President was empowered to appoint the following six Committees.

The President appointed.

LAWRENCE VERDON, MICH.,
P. A. SINNOTT, Mass.,
Capt. THOS. K. BARRETT, Ills.,
W. J. HYNES, Mass.,
J. C. O'BRIEN, N. Y.,
THOMAS HAIRE, Ills.,
J. W. FITZGERALD, Ohio,
JOHN A. GEARY, Ky.,
} Committee on Foreign Affairs.

MILES J. O'REILLY, Mich.,
B. HIGGINS, N. Y.,
P. A. COLLINS, Mass.,
THOMAS McCARTHY, Tenn.,
THOS. HURLEY, N. Y.,
JAMES McDERMOTT, Central Organizer.
P. F. WALSH,   do
J. J. ROGERS, N. Y.,
A. WYNNE, Penna.,
} Committee on Government Constitution and By-Laws.

P. W. DUNNE, Ills.,
PATRICK GIBBONS, Iowa,
P. BANNON, Ky.,
MORTIMER SCANLAN, Ills.,
PATRICK KEENAN, N. Y.,
WM. MORAN, Mo.,
} Committee on Ways and Means and Finances.

A. L. MORRISON, Ills.,
J. P. HODNETT, N. J.,
J. F. FINNERTY, Ills.,
} Com. on Address to Ireland.

JAMES GIBBONS, Penna.,
Capt. P. F. WALSH, "
H. O'C. McCARTHY, Deputy H. C.
} Committee on Address to America.

Col. W. G. HALPIN, Army of Cumberland.
JAMES McDERMOTT, Ky.,
} Committee on Resolutions.

In compliance with Col. Mullen's resolution of yesterday, the chair appointed the following:

Col. S. J. McGROARTY, Ohio,
" B. F. MULLEN, Ind.,
" JOHN H. GLEASON, Army of Potomac,
Lieut. Col. P. J. DOWNING, N. J.,
" " PATRICK LEONARD, N. Y.,
Major MATTHEW DONOVAN, Mass.,
Capt. MICHAEL BAILEY, N. Y.,
" JOSEPH POLLARD, R. I.,
" MICHAEL SCANLAN, Mass.,
" CORNELIUS O'BRIEN, Conn.,
" HUGH RODGERS, Penn.,
" P. K. WALSH, Ohio,
" THOS. FUREY, Penna.,

Committee on Military Affairs.

On motion of M. Scanlan, the Deputy H. C. read a letter from the C. E. of the I. R. B. omitting a personal passage, which upon motion was passed over.

Upon motion it was resolved that so much of the letter of the C. E. as relates to the time for the commencement of hostilities, be and the same is hereby referred to the Committee on Military Affairs.

Upon motion it was resolved that the Committee on Ways and Means be instructed to enquire into and report upon the most practicable plan of raising immediately the greatest amount of funds to aid the work of Revolution in Ireland.

The books of the "Chicago Irish National Fair," were presented to the house and were referred to the Committee on Finance.

Upon motion it was " resolved that so much of the address of the H. C. as relates to the duties of committees be read to the house before their retirement.

The Committee then retired.

Upon motion, it was resolved, that so much of the Envoy's Report as relates to the cost of arms in Ireland, the kind and quantity of ordnance and ordnance stores, now in the possession of the I. R. B., and all matters pertaining to the I. R. B., as a military organization, be referred to the Military Committee.

On motion, it was resolved, that H. O'C. McCarthy be added to the Finance Committe.

On motion, it was resolved, that the rules be suspended, and that an extra session be held at night, commencing at 7½ o'clock.

Congress then adjourned to meet again at 2 o'clock, P. M.

Afternoon Session.

At 2 o'clock the President called the Congress to order.

On motion, the calling of the Roll was dispensed with.

Richard Doherty, Ind., Treasurer of the O'Flaherty Monument Committee, reported on that subject, which report was on motion adopted.

After considerable debate, the O'Flaherty Monument Committee was ordered to prosecute its work to completion.

The Chairman of the Committee on Address to Ireland, read the address drawn up by it. Adopted unanimously.

A vote of thanks was upon motion, tendered to the Committee.

At 5¼ o'clock the Congress adjourned to meet again at 7½ o'clock, P. M.

Night Session.

At 7½ o'clock, P. M. the President called the Congress to order.

The Deputy H. C., informed the house that the various committees would be able to present their reports at 10 o'clock, P. M.

On motion, it was resolved that no member be allowed to leave the hall until after the reports were submitted.

The Congress then took a recess for one half hour. On re-assembling, the Military Committee, through its Chairman, Colonel B. F. Mullen, submitted the report of that Committee.

A Minority Report of this Committee, was also presented by Lieut. Col. Downing.

On motion, both reports were accepted.

R. Doherty, Ind., moved that both reports be laid on the table. Lost

H. O'C. McCarthy, proposed the following resolution:

Resolved. That the Reports of Military Committees be accepted, but that they be sent to the C. E. of the I. R. B., for his approval before being put in force, and that the time for military organization be determined by the progress of affairs in Ireland, the suggestion of said time being made by the C. E. through the Head Centre of the F. B.

Seconded and carried.

The report of the Committee on Foreign Affairs, was presented and adopted. The following is a digest of the report:

The Committee on Foreign Affairs, of the Fenian Brotherhood, in Convention at Cincinnati, Ohio, January 19th, 1865, respectfully report:

   *   *   *   *   *   *

   *   *   *   *   *   *   *

   *   *   *   *   *   ⅄ ◄   *

FIRST,   *   *   *   *   *   *

   *   *   *   *   *   *   *

   *   *   *   *   *   *   *

SECOND, That we recommend all members of the Fenian Brotherhood to aid in giving the widest possible circulation to the "Irish People" newspaper; and that every delegate of this Convention be especially urged to contribute by his influence and personal efforts, to its support, as its continuance is regarded of vital importance to the National cause.

THIRD, That in view of information just received from the report of our Envoy to Europe, we are convinced of the ability of the I. R. B., if furnished with aid sufficient from America, to carry to a successful issue the work before them.

Fourth, Considering the fearful tide of emigration from our native land, we cannot hope, in the event of failure in this movement, that the people of Ireland would ever be able to inaugurate and mature another; and bearing in mind also, the past exertions and present condition of the organization at present existing in Ireland, we do consider it our holy and imperative duty to give it our entire support, limited only by impossibilities.

Fifth,   *   *   *   *   *   *

    *   *   *   *   ′   *   *   *

    *   *   *   *   *   *   *

Sixth,   *   *   *   *   *   *

    *   *   *   *   *   *   *

    *   *   *   *   *   *   *

Seventh, We are of opinion, that it would be exceedingly unsafe to establish communication with the I. R. B., otherwise than through the Head Centre; and, we reprobate the practice of communication between the unauthorized members of the F. B., with their friends in Ireland or elsewhere on matters pertaining to the organization.

The Committee on Finance reported through its Chairman, P. W. Dunne. The report, after some discussion, was unanimously adopted. The following are extracts from this report:

" The Fiancial Committee beg leave to report, that they have thoroughly examined all the books and documents appertaining to the Central Financial Affairs of the Fenian Brotherhood, and have found them strictly correct and satisfactory.

" The Committee have also, examined the books and accounts of the Executive Committee of the late Irish National Fair, in Chicago; and, with the exception of a clerical error, have found them correct and satisfactory.

" The Financial Committee suggest, in view of the increasing revenue of the organization, and in view also, of the onerous requirements which may soon fall upon that department, that it be placed in the hands of a responsible man of first-class ability.

" And they recommend, that in view of the pressing and well supported call of the I. R. B., there be made an immediate levy of $5 upon each member in the various circles. Each circle should be pledged to make up a sum equal in amount to the rate of $5 per member for each member of the circle. This will create a revenue that will supply fully the immediate want, and will convince the members of the I. R. B., that we are up to a sense of our responsibility and duty. No cessation of dues should result from this call. Each member should contribute his regular quota.

" All officers and delegates in this Congress should be notified to the effect that upon their return to their respective circles, they begin at once the collection. The entire levy should be on its way to the Central Treasurer, within ten days from the date of adjournment, if possible. The Committee also, suggest that the Department of Finance issue regularly each week a printed list of the subscriptions received on this call. to every circle in good standing in the Brotherhood. Also, that hereafter printed circulars of receipts from the various circles be issued to the same, by the Financial Department, on the 10th of each month.

" The Committee would submit to the Congress, with deference to its action and approval, their opinion that the financial suggestions with reference to the special levy, cannot be acted upon too soon, for the *morale* of the I. R. B. Also, that if another special call be made by the C. E. of the I. R. B., the Head Centre of the Fenian Brotherhood is hereby authorized to enforce the same.

*   *   *   *   *   *   *

" The Committee would also suggest, that the circles now engaged earnestly in acquiring revolutionary funds, should go on with that work, so far as they are capable ; as the calls which may be made upon them, may come unexpectedly and quickly.

" This Committee also respectfully suggest, that all financial communications be addressed to the Central Treasurer, and that the Central Treasurer be put under such amount of bonds as the Executive and Central Council shall determine. We recommend that a Financial Secretary, a Fenian, and a man of first-class business ability be selected for that office.

" The Finance Committee respectfully submit that, after the report of the Committee on Government and Constitution and By-Laws be adopted, they will then report an *addenda*, suggesting the compensation to which the various officers should be entitled.

" Your Committee would further recommend, that in view of the great responsibilities attached to the office of the Executive in New York, and inasmuch as the health of our worthy brother and late Deputy H. C., will not permit of his uninterrupted attention to our interests, that he shall have the full supervision and control of the financial officers and affairs as it may best suit his convenience."

The Congress, on motion, adjourned at 12 o'clock, (night,) to meet at 9 o'clock, A. M., on Friday, January 20th.

Fourth Day's Session.

FRIDAY, JANUARY 20, 1865.

At 9 o'clok, A. M., the President called the Congress to order.

The minutes of the previous session were read by the Secretary, which upon motion, were adopted.

The Committee on Government, Constitution and By-Laws, reported through its Chairman. The report was accepted and upon motion, ordered to be adopted by paragraphs.

Upon motion it was ordered, that no member be allowed to leave the hall during the discussion and adoption of the Constitution and By-Laws.

The Congress adjourned at 1 o'clock, P. M., for one hour.

Afternoon Session.

The President called the Congress to order at 2 o'clock, P. M.

The report of the Committee on Government, Constitution and By-Laws being under discussion was continued.

On motion the rules were suspended for the purpose of introducing an *addenda* report from the Committee on Foreign Affairs.

The report was read by J. C. O'Brien, N. Y., and adopted.

On motion, it was ordered that a copy of the report, signed by the Committee, be presented to the officers of the Indianapolis, Indiana Circle.

The report of the Committee on Government, Constitution and By-Laws was again taken up and adopted by paragraphs.

On motion, it was adopted as a whole.

On motion, a vote of thanks was presented to the Committee for their labors.

The Committee on Address to the People of America, presented the address prepared by them.

The address with some slight amendments was adopted as a whole.

On motion a vote of thanks was presented to the Committee.

The Finance Committee presented an *addenda* report which was, upon motion, adopted unanimously.

The Committee on Resolutions, reported a series of Resolutions, which are as follows:—

Resolutions of Second Fenian Congress.

I.

WHEREAS, Since our last Congress, the hand of death has deprived us of the gallant General Michael Corcoran, a member of our Central Council, and one of the principal founders of, and most indefatigable workers in this organization,

Be it Resolved, That while reverently submitting to the Will of God, we deeply feel the heavy loss to our holy cause, of a patriot so earnest and influential, and of a soldier so able and illustrious; and while we profoundly sympathize with the friends and fellow-countrymen of our departed brother, in mourning his loss, we feel assured that his noble example will only excite them to increased love of the principles which he cherished, and to more determined devotedness to the cause which he so faithfully served.

II.

WHEREAS, Having thoroughly and scrupulously investigated the official action of the Head Centre, the Deputy Head Centre, and Central Council of the Fenian Brotherhood, during the last fourteen months,

Be it Resolved, That we feel bound to bear our most decided testimony to the ability, integrity and patriotic devotedness wherewith their onerous and responsible duties have been discharged; and, that on the part of the Fenian Brotherhood we individually and collectively express to them our unshaken confidence, and congratulating them on the gratifying success which has hitherto crowned their efforts, we tender to them our sincere and grateful thanks.

III.

WHEREAS, Having had personal evidence, the most reliable and satisfactory, of the progress of our principles amongst our brothers at home, be it,

Resolved, That we place the most unlimited confidence in the distinguished talents and honorable character of the C. E. I. R. B., to whom we hereby tender our earnest and undivided support.

IV.

WHEREAS, It is the profound conviction of this Second Congress of the F. B., that immediate and vigorous action is absolutely essential to carry on our work to a speedy and successful issue, be it,

Resolved, That it is the incumbent and imperative duty of every member of the organization, who would prove his real earnestness in the work he professes to have undertaken, to act vigorously on the advice of this Congress, and to respond with promptitude and liberality to the special call for an immediate subsidy which has been made by the authority of Congress.

V.

WHEREAS, Since the commencement of the present civil war in America, and more especially since our last Congress, the Fenian Brotherhood has lost a large number of its most valuable members who, as officers and men, perished on the battle-field while defending the integrity of their adopted country, be it

Resolved, That while we deeply deplore the heavy loss sustained by the cause of Irish freedom, in the untimely fall of so many of its most effective and patriotic assertors, we, at the same time, are permitted to enjoy the melancholy pleasure of proclaiming our unqualified admiration of their bravery and loyalty as soldiers of the American republic. Be it further

Resolved, That, in order to procure some memorial of the services of our late lamented brothers, the Head Centre be instructed to draw up a roll of all members of the Fenian Brotherhood, who, so far as it can be ascertained, have laid down their lives for the American Union, since the beginning of the present conflict, and that said Roll shall be deposited at Head Quarters, in the Archives of this Organization.

P. W. Dunne, of Ills., offered a resolution relating to "Our Native Land," which was adopted unanimously and with acclamation.

James Gibbons, Penna., offered the following resolution, which was unanimously adopted:

Resolved, That this Congress express the most implicit confidence in the patriotism and earnestness of our brothers in California, and in the ability and wisdom of the State Centre and officers generally of the Brotherhood in that noble State; and, that we implore them to enforce faithfully the laws enacted by this Congress, and especially in connection with the special call.

Patrick Gibbons, Keokuk, Iowa, offered the following resolution, which was adopted:

Resolved, That should any member of this Congress have come here with either doubt, suspicion or scepticism as to the efficient working of the Fenian Brotherhood, we, the members, after the most searching scrutiny, are convinced that all such were quite groundless, and we hereby declare them removed. That we further proclaim our fullest confidence in the ability, patriotism, and integrity of its management; and, in our capacity as delegates, we say to our constituents BE OF GOOD CHEER! ALL IS WELL!!

On motion, John O'Mahony, of N. Y. City, was unanimously re-elected Head Centre for the year 1865, amid the most vociferous acclamations.

Col. O'Mahony accepted the position, and after making a short address, cheers, three times three, were given for "O'Mahony and McCarthy!"

On motion, the marked thanks of Congress was presented to the Deputy Head Centre, Henry O'Clarence McCarthy, and to the Central Council of 1864.

The H. C., then nominated the following gentlemen for the Central Council of 1865

JAMES GIBBONS, Penna.,
H O'C. McCARTHY,
P. BANNON, Ky.,
P. W. DUNNE, Ills.,
WILLAM GRIFFIN, Ind.,

Brigadier General THOMAS A. SMYTH,
Army of the Potomac,
MICHEL SCANLAN, Ills.,
WM. SULLIVAN, Ohio.

The H. C., also appointed Patrick O'Rourke, N. Y., Central Treasurer, Patrick Keenan, Assistant Central Treasurer.

All the nominations were unanimously ratified by the Congress.

P. O'Rourke offered his resignation, thanking the President and the House for the compliment.

The resignation was declined by the H. C., and unanimously rejected by the Congress.

P. A. Collins, offered a resolution amendatory of the Constitution, which was laid on the table.

On motion, the different State delegations went into caucusses for the election of their respective States Centres.

On their return, the following names were presented to the President for general ratification:

STATE CENTRES:

Massachusetts,..............DANIEL DONOVAN, Lawrence,
Illinois,.....................MICHAEL SCANLAN, Chicago,
New York, (State).........D. O'SULLIVAN, Auburn,
Manhattan, (Dept.,)......JAMES J. ROGERS, New York City,
Indiana,....................BERNARD B. DALY, Delphi,
Pennsylvania,..............JAMES GIBBONS, Philadelphia,
Ohio,....... ....JAMES W. FITZGERALD, Cincinnati,
Kentucky,..................P. BANNON, Louisville,
Missouri,....................JAMES McGRATH. St, Louis,
Iowa,...........................PATRICK GIBBONS, Keokuk,
Wisconsin,...................JOHN A. BYRNE, Madison,
Michigan,.....................MILES J. O'REILLY, Detroit,
California,....................JEREMIAH KAVANAGH, San Francisco.
New Hampshire,...........CORNELIUS HEALY, Manchester,
District of Columbia,.....P. H. DONEGAN, Washington,
Army of the Potomac,...THOS. A. SMYTH, Brig. Gen.

On motion the appointment of State Centres for Tennessee, New Jersey, Connecticut, Kansas, and Minnesota, was referred to the Head Centre and Central Council.

On motion the marked thanks of the Congress were tendered to the Central Organizers:—Capt. P. F. Walsh, of Penna., James Brennan, of N. Y., W. J. Hynes, of N. E., J. W. O'Brien, of Iowa, and James McDermott, of N. Y.

Votes of thanks were also presented to the Vice Presidents,—and to the Cincinnati Circle of the F. B., and its Centre J. W. Fitzgerald, for their generous proposal to defray the expenses of the convention.

On the suggestion of M. Scanlan, Ill., the subject of the Fenian Sisterhood, was referred to the H. C. and Central Council.

On motion the Secretaries were instructed to condense reports of the proceedings of the Congress for the Irish and Irish-American newspapers.

H. O'C. McCarthy moved that the H. C., and Central Council be instructed .and empowered to get printed in pamphlet form the proceedings of Congress, with the new Government Constitution and By-Laws, and that copies be forwarded to every Circle in the country; seconded and carried.

The Congress then adjourned *sine die.*

APPENDIX.

Extract from minutes of proceedings of the Central Council, F. B., held at Head Quarters, September 27th, 1864.

Upon motion it was resolved "that Cincinnati, Ohio, be the place selected for the next annual convention of the Fenian Brotherhood."

Upon motion it was resolved " that the preliminary meeting take place on Tuesday, January 17th, 1865, at 10 o'clock, A. M., and that the following regulations be observed:"

All circles to be represented in convention should be in "good standing," having communicated and reported to the proper officers for the month of November, 1864.   Circles will be notified from Head Quarter's when to elect delegates, and how many certificates will be furnished in blank to each circle, which will be filled out by the proper officers for Centre and Delegate. Without this certificate no person can be admitted either into the preliminary meeting or into the Convention.

All officers will bring with them their commissions.

Circles represented by proxies will cause their presiding officers to forward their commissions by mail to Head Quarters.

Details connected with the above will reach the Circles through an official circular.

CONSTITUTION
OF THE
FENIAN BROTHERHOOD,
As amended and adopted in Second Annual Congress,
AT CINCINNATI, OHIO, JANUARY 1865.

I.

The FENIAN BROTHERHOOD is a DISTINCT and INDEPENDENT organization.

It is composed, in the first place, of citizens of the United States of America of Irish birth and lineage ; and, in the second place, of Irish men and of Friends of Ireland living on the American Continent and in the Provinces of the British Empire, wherever situated.

Its Head-quarters are and shall be within the limits of the United States of America.

II.

Its members are bound together by the following
GENERAL PLEDGE.

I,——— ——— ———solemnly pledge my sacred word of honor as a truthful and honest man, that I will labor with earnest zeal for the liberation of Ireland from the yoke of England, and for the establishment of a Free and Independent Government on the Irish soil ; that I will implicitly obey the commands of my superior officers in the Fenian Brotherhood in all things appertaining to my duties as a member thereof ; that I will faithfully discharge my duties of membership as laid down in the Constitution and By Laws thereof ; that I will do my utmost to promote feelings of love, harmony and kindly forbearance among all Irishmen ; and that I will foster, defend and propagate the aforesaid Fenian Brotherhood to the utmost of my power.

III.

FORM OF ORGANIZATION.

The Fenian Brotherhood shall be sub-divided into State organizations and Circles.

It shall be directed and governed by a Head Centre, to direct the whole organization ; State Centres to direct State organizations and Centres to direct Circles.

The Head Centre shall be assisted by a Central Council of ten ; by a Central Treasurer, and assistant Treasurer ; by a Central Corresponding Secretary and a Central Financial Secretary ; and by such intermediate officers as the Head Centre with the advice and consent of the Central Council, may from time to time, deem necessary for the efficient working of the organization.

IV.
THE HEAD CENTRE.

The Head Centre shall be elected annually by a General Congress of the Fenian Brotherhood, which Congress shall be composed of the State Centres, and one delegate from each Circle in good standing and containing less than one hundred members, and one additional delegate from each Circle in good standing and containing more than one hundred members.

A Circle to be in good standing must have made regular and satisfactory reports through its Centre, to its State Centre and Head Centre, within a period of nine weeks previous to a General Congress.

V.
THE CENTRAL COUNCIL.

The Central council shall consist of ten members, who shall be nominated by the Head Centre, and elected at a General Congress.

The Central Council shall have powers to elect from their own members a President and such other officers as they may deem necessary for the business of the Council.

In case of the death, resignation, removal or refusal to act, of the Head Centre, the President of the Central Council shall have all the powers and prerogatives, and perform all the duties of Head Centre, and be obeyed and respected as such, until the convening of the next General Congress.

The Central Council shall have power to call a Convention of State Centres, or a General Congress whenever they may deem it necessary for the transaction of extraordinary business. Such Convention of State Centres or such General Congress shall have the power of impeaching and removing any officer in the organization.

The Central Council shall have power to examine and audit the accounts of the Head Centre and Central Treasurer, and all financial transactions of the Brotherhood or any part thereof, The Central Council shall report to the annual Congress.

VI.
THE CENTRAL TREASURER, ASSISTANT CENTRAL TREASURER, CENTRAL CORRESPONDING SECRETARY AND CENTRAL FINANCIAL SECRETARY.

The Central Treasurer and the Assistant Treasurer shall be nominated by the Head Centre and elected at a General Congress.

The Central Treasurer shall be required to furnish bonds in such manner as the Head Centre and Central Council may direct in order to secure to the pecuniary interests of the Fenian Brotherhood an efficient protection.

The Head Centre may, with the consent of the Central Council, remove the Central Treasurer.

The Central Treasurer shall pay to the order of the Head Centre, provided the disbursements be for the objects of the Fenian Brotherhood, such sums as he may have funded of the moneys of the Brotherhood; but he shall retain explanatory receipts as vouchers therefor, in order to exhibit a clear financial statement to the Central Council.

The Central Secretaries above designated shall be appointed by the Head Centre, by and with the advice and consent of the Central Council.

VII.
STATE CENTRES.

State Centres upon the recommendation of the majority of representatives of the respective States who shall be present at the annual Congress shall be appointed and commissioned by the Head Centre, who shall also have the power of rejecting the appointment, and with the assent of the Central Council of changing or appointing State Centres.

The State Centre shall supervise the organization in his State. He shall establish Circles and communicate with all parties therein who desire instruction or advice. He shall on the tenth of each month make to the Head Centre a consolidated report, thoroughly explanatory of the condition of the organization of his State.

He shall with the approval of the H. C. and C. C. mark out a route in his State for an agent to traverse, with instructions to canvass and organize the same.

VIII.
CENTRES.

Centres shall be elected by Circles, and after the approval of the Head Centre shall be commissioned by the State Centre; each commission being countersigned by the Head Centre.

The Centre shall preside at all regular meetings of his Circle, and shall report upon the 25th of each month to the State Centre, setting forth the increase or decrease in his Circle with names and the average attendance of members, the amount of money received, the amount disbursed for local expenditures, specifying each item, with the balance remitted, on the 25th to the Head Centre. One copy of this report shall be sent to the State Centre, one copy thereof shall be transmitted to the Head Centre, with the remittance for the month; and one copy thereof shall be retained by the Circle for future reference.

Any Circle or Centre not reporting to the State Centre, as above required, for the space of three months may be declared in bad standing, and be cut off from the organization by order of the State Centre, with the approval of the Head Centre and Central Council.

IX.
PRESIDING OFFICERS.

In the absence of the Centre, the Chairman of the Committee of Safety shall preside at business meetings.

X.
OFFICERS OF CIRCLES.

A Treasurer shall be nominated and elected by each Circle. It shall be his duty to receive and account for all moneys appertaining to his Circle, to make up a Financial Report, on the 25th of each month. The balance on hand he shall forward to the Head Centre on the same stated day every month, without fail.

A Secretary shall be nominated and elected by each Circle. It shall be his duty to make a faithful record of the proceedings of each meeting ; he shall keep the financial accounts and sign the official reports of his Circle, and shall in all things comport himself in accordance with the established duties of a Secretary.

A Committee of Safety, consisting of not less than three nor more than seven members, shall be nominated by the Centre and elected at a regular meeting of the Circle. This committee shall have the power of receiving members, together with the power of expelling them ; but, in each case their action must be submitted for approval to a meeting of their Circle. A vote of want of confidence in the Committee of Safety, will necessitate the immediate resignation of its members.

XI.
ADMISSION OF MEMBERS.

Every candidate for admission into the Fenian Brotherhood, must be proposed one week before initiation.

XII.
MEMBERS IN GOOD STANDING.

Members in good standing are alone entitled to a voice in matters of business.

XIII.
MEMBERS IN BAD STANDING.

Members who have not attended a meeting of their Circle, or whose dues shall remain unpaid for thirteen successive weeks, when their absence or failure to pay is not accounted for by a legitimate excuse, shall be considered *in bad standing*, and their names shall be stricken from the Roll of the Fenian Brotherhood.

No member *in bad standing* shall enter into a Fenian Circle whatever until he has shown to the Committee of Safety of his previous Circle, sufficient cause to satisfy them of his firm resolve to act thenceforward the part of a truthful and steadfast Fenian.

Previous to his re-admission into the Brotherhood, he shall pay a fine of not less than one dollar, and shall clear up all arrears of his weekly dues.

XIV.
MEETINGS.

Each Circle of the Fenian Brotherhood shall meet once a week, for the transaction of business, at such time and place as may be deemed most in accordance with their interests and convenience.

All discussions upon religious, or upon political matters foreign to the cause of Irish nationality, shall be peremptorily excluded from every meeting of the Fenian Brotherhood.

Any presiding officer who shall violate or suffer to be violated the foregoing provision, shall be deposed.

XV.
DUES AND INITIATION FEES.

The weekly dues of each member shall not be less than ten cents, nor shall the Initiation Fee be less than one dollar.

Each Circle can however, increase the rate of dues and initiation fee, in accordance with the devotion and ability of its members.

XVI.
' RELATIONS OF MEMBERS AND OFFICERS.

' Centres will correspond with, report to, and be directed by their State Centre.

State Centres will correspond with, report to, and be directed by the Head Centre.

No correspondence whatever can be held with Ireland or Europe on the business of the organization, except through the Head Centre. No communications on that business can be received in the United States from abroad except through the Head Centre. Any member or officer derogating from this law shall be considered a traitor.

XVII.
PERFIDY.

Perfidy on the part of a member, shall be punished by expulsion.

Maligning the objects of the organization, calumniating its officers or members ; conveying information to the enemy ; or, injuring seriously the organization by disgraceful conduct or conversation, shall constitute Perfidy.

The names and description of all persons guilty of Perfidy, shall be sent by the Head Centre to all Circles throughout the United States, to be there kept on record.

XVIII.
MEN COMING FROM ABROAD.

Men coming from abroad who represent themselves to be members of the I.R.B. before they are admitted into any Circle must first be recognized by the Head Centre, and referred to the State Centre of the State in which they intend to reside.

Where it is difficult to obtain this recognition, the Centre to whom the party applies, shall forward information and documents to the State Centre, who will advise him in the case ; otherwise the applicant must be proposed in the regular manner, and initiated as a new member.

XIX.
CARDS AND LETTERS OF INTRODUCTION.

When members change localities they shall carry a letter of introduction and a certificate from the Centre of the Circle to which they had been attached, to the Centre of the Circle to which they are going. This will be taken up on presentation, and reported back to the Centre who issued it; and, when found correct, the bearer thereof shall be received as a member.

In places where Circles are very large, cards may be issued to identify members; but, such cards, themselves, will in no case entitle a member to admission into any circle other than that from which the card is issued.

XX.
ELECTIONS AND TERMS OF OFFICE.

All the elected officers of the several State organizations and Circles of the Fenian Brotherhood, shall hold office for a period of one year from the date of their commissions, unless in case of death, resignation or dismissal. In either of these contingencies, the successor shall hold office for the residue of the unexpired term.

XXI.
RESIGNATIONS AND DISMISSALS.

Resignations, to be valid, must in the first instance, be received by a majority of the Circle of the resigning officer, and next forwarded by his immediate superior to the Head Centre for approval.

Any officer of the Fenian Brotherhood may be dismissed from his position for perfidy, neglect of duty, disobedience of legitimate orders, by a decree of his immediate superior in command, or by a two-thirds vote of his constituents, subject however, in case of appeal, to the approval of the Head Centre, and a majority of the Central Council.

XXII.
JURISDICTION OF THE HEAD CENTRE AND CENTRAL COUNCIL.

The decision of the Head Centre, shall, with the written consent of a majority of the members of the Central Council be absolute and conclusive upon all points that are not specially provided for in these By-Laws, until the next annual Congress of the Fenian Brotherhood.

XXIII
ANNUAL CONRESS.

A Congress of the Fenian Brotherhood shall be held annually, during the month of January of each year, until the Independence of Ireland shall be established. The election of a Head Centre, Central Council, Central Treasurer, and Assistant Treasurer, for the ensuing year, shall be held at the said annual Congress.

It shall receive and confirm reports of the progress, strength and pecuniary resources of the Fenian Brotherhood during the current year, and shall make such alterations in its Constitution and By-Laws as may be found necessary for its more efficient working.

The said annual Congress shall be held within the limits of the United States of America, at such place as shall seem fit to the Head Centre and Cen. tral Council.

XXIV.

RESOLUTIONS OF THE FIRST FENIAN CONGRESS.

The Resolutions passed on the fourth day of November, 1863, by the First Fenian Congress held in the city of Chicago, and State of Illinois, and, after mature deliberation, signed by the Centres and Delegates there assembled, as amended by the resolutions of the Second Fenian Congress, held in the city of Cincinnatti, and the State of Ohio, on the seventeenth day of January, 1865, are, and shall be adopted as part of the Constitution and By-Laws of the Fenian Brotherhood.

XXV.

LOCAL BY-LAWS.

Each Circle shall have the power of enacting By-Laws for its special government. These shall be brief and comprehensive, and shall in no way conflict with the Constitution and By-Laws of the Fenian Brotherhood.

A Special Committee shall prepare the said Local By-Laws, which shall then be submitted to the Circle for their approval.

ORDER OF BUSINESS.

1. Order.
2. Roll call.
3. Initiation of new members,
4. Reading of minutes.
5. Collection of dues and fines.
6. Reports of committees and officers.
7. Reading of correspondence.
8. Propoposition of new members.
9. Unfinished business.
10. New business.
11. Patriotic readings.
12. Adjournment.

BLANK FORM OF MONTHLY REPORT.

.◆........................ DISTRICT OF THE FENIAN BROTHERHOOD.

MONTHLY REPORT of the .... *Circle of the Fenian Brotherhood,* .... 186.

Meeting.	No. Present.	Increase.	Decrease.	Amount of Dues &c., Received.	Amount of cash paid, (setting forth items, time, amount, and for what.)	
				$ cts.	Date	$ cts.
1st.						
2d.						
3d.						
4th.						
5th						

Total Amount Received,

Actual Strength of Circle, ...

Disbursed for Local Ependitures,

Balance remited to H. C.

Total remitted to date,

.... *Secretary*,

.... *Treasurer.*

Names and causes of expulsion or desertion. ‖ Remarks

...., *Centre.*

John O'Mahony, New York City,
Henry O'C. McCarthy,   "
P. W. Dunne, Peoria, Ill.,
P. Bannon, Louisville, Ky.,
Michael Scanlan, Chicago, Ill.,
James Gibbons, Philadelphia, Pa.,
T. B. Hennesey, Boston, Mass.,
P. A. Collins,   "   "
Patrick Keenan,   "   "
P. A. Sinnott,   "   "
Pat'k. McDonough, "   "
Jeremiah Buckley, "   "
Capt. J. M. Tóbin, "   "

E. J. Flaherty, Boston, Mass.,
David Powers, Springfield, "
William J. Hynes, "   "
Matthew Donovan, Lowell, "
R. C. Fanning, Chelsea,   "
Thomas Sinnott, Spencer. "
Capt. T. R. Rourke, Dedham, "
Capt. M. A. Finnerty,   "   "
D. O'Donovan, Haverhill,   "
John Morrisey, Ware,   "
Bernard Connelly, Lynn,   "
C. A. Mangan, Summerville, "
M. S. McConville, Worcester, "

John Brennan, Brighton, Mass.,
Matthew Foley, Stoneham, "
J.J.McDonnell, Winchenden,"
P. Forristal, Haydenville, "
Jere'h. Egan, Greenfield, "
Dan'l. Donovan, Lawrence, "
Thomas Doody, Holyoke, "
Richard Lynch, " "
R. M. Fahey, Hopkinton, "
James Costegan, " "
Florence McGill, Natick, "
Charles Gallagher, Taunton,"
Frank A. O'Hara, Chicopee,"
Thomas Stafford, Brookline,"
M. A. O'Brien, Charleston, "
T. Hurley, South Reading, "
M. C. McGuire, Boston, "
John L. White, " "
Thos. F. Robinson, Concord, N. H.,
O. J. Varley, Wilton, "
Cornelius Healy, Manchester, "
Peter Fahey, " "
P. M. O'Grady, Claremont, "
Patrick J. Flaherty, Nashua, "
Michael G. Cole, Dover, "
M. Hartnett, Exeter, "
Patrick O'Malley, Providence, R. I.
Capt. Joseph Pollard, " "
Charles O'Neill, Peace Dale, "
James O'Reilly, Woonsockett, '
John Hogan, " "
John McLoughlin, Greenville, "
James Burke, Valley Falls, "
Wm. Hagerty, West Meriden, Conn.,
William Heshen, Waterbury, "
William Delany, Hartford, "
M. Carlin, " "
Daniel Carroll, New Haven, "
Capt. O'Brien, " "
E. H. Perry, New London, "
John Lonergan, Burlington, Vt.
Patrick O'Rourke, New York City,
James J. Rogers, "
James McDermott, "
James Brennan, "
Michael Cavanagh, "
Patrick Cooney, "
William R. Roberts, "
James H. O'Neill, "
John Rafferty, "
Patrick Keenan, "
Joseph McGloue, "
P. Fitzwilliams, "
Anthony McOwen, "
John O'Brien, "
T. T. Corkery, "

John F. Fitzsimmons, New York City,
Lt. Col. Patrick, Leonard, "
Capt. B. P. Murphy, Brooklyn, N. Y.
Michael Kennedy, Troy, "
John McKenna, " "
William Flemming, " "
John Stanton, " "
Thomas Hurley, " "
Timothy Dohan, " "
Capt. Owen Gavigan, Auburn. "
Daniel O'Sullivan, " "
John Barrett, Dunkirk, "
P. N. Madigan, " "
Charles J. Burke, Rochester, "
J. C. O'Brien, " "
William McCarthy, " "
Michael McCarthy, Elmira, "
William Sullivan, " "
John Gorman, Syracuse, "
Thomas Byrne, " "
Daniel Cahill, Watertown, "
T. Flanigan, Saratoga Springs, "
E. J. Maurice, Malone, "
Bartholomew Higgins, Waterford, "
Terence J. Quinn, Albany, "
James McShea, " "
Michael Clarke, Saugerties, "
P. Olwell, Schenectady, "
W. P. McKinley, Oswego, "
Capt. J. Joyce, " "
William O'Dwyer, Herkimer, "
Thomas White, " "
William Walsh, Brockport, "
T. McDonnell, Cooperstown, "
Thomas O'Reilly, Yonkers, "
Capt. M. O'Reilly, Seneca Falls, "
Jeremiah Faunt, " "
Michael Monaghan, Cohoes, "
Peter J. Brennan, Utica, "
Capt. M. Baily, Buffalo, "
John C. Canty, " "
Patrick O'Day, " "
Lt. Col. P. J. Downing, Newark, N. J.
J. Kelley, " "
John Pope Hodnett, Jersey City, "
Francis J. Mitchell, " "
P. F. Walsh, Philadelphia, Pa.,
Andrew Wynne, " "
J. Bergin, " " •
J. Monaghan, " "
M. Caville, " "
John Brennan, " "
Martin Brennan, " "
Hugh Rogers, " "
Capt. Furey, " "
Daniel Terry, Pittsburgh, "

Cornelius Murphy, Pittsburg, Pa.
John L. Byrne, Broadtop, "
Andrew Gleason, " "
R. A. Costello, Meadville, "
Charles E. Collins, Altoona, "
D. Fogarty, Erie, "
John Reynolds, Warren, "
S. G. Wright, Lockhaven, "
Maurice Lundy Williamsport, "
James Connolly, Danville, "
J. W. Fitzgerald, Cin., Ohio,
J. B. Maurice, " "
John N. Hayes, " "
Thomas McDowell, " "
William Sullivan, Tiffin, "
John Britt, " "
J. Manning, Cleveland, "
P. K. Walsh, " "
J. McNamara, " "
Patrick Moncks, " "
Andrew Fagan, " "
John Casey, Lancaster, "
James Monaghan, " "
B. Cusick, Marion, "
Philip O'Neill, " "
T. Confoy, Youngstown, "
T. O'Mahony, Columbus, "
J. Hannegan, Richwood, "
Philip Hussey, " "
P. C. Noonan, Ackron, "
E. J. Kinsella, " "
Dan'l. Donovan, Crestline, "
E. O'Brien, Dayton, "
Connor Alcock, Hudson, "
J. Quinn, Toledo, "
J. McNamara, Mansfield, "
Richard Doherty, Lafayette, Indiana,
Robert Shealy, " "
Richard O'Meara, " "
F. J. Grant, " "
Owen McSweeny, " "
Thomas Brennan, " "
Bernard B. Daily, Delphi, "
Dr. Anthony Garrett, " "
Daniel McCarthy, Richmond, "
Patrick B. Hynes, " "
Morgan Kane, Mitchel, "
John O'Donnell, " "
William Boland, " "
James T. More, Terre Haute, "
Martin Grace, " "
Thomas Nash, Indianapolis, "
John Shields, " "
J. Austen Stewart, " "
John Redmond, " "
Thomas Redmond, " "
John Waldron, Bloomington, "
Terence McSweeny, " "
John Tighe, New Albany, "

John Kane, Logansport, Indiana,
Thomas Rodgers, Aurora, "
Michael Maloney, " "
John Cawley, Greencastle, "
M. Naughton, Jeffersonville, "
Martin Johnson, Shelbyville, "
Capt. John Keily, La Porte, "
Capt. John Scully, " "
Thomas Brennan, Lafayette, "
Patrick Davy, " "
P. Byrne, Madison, "
Wm. Griffin, " "
Michael O'Connell, Bedford, "
Daniel Lynch, Columbus, "
William P. Bayne, " "
John Carroll, Crawfordsville, "
G. W. McWilliams, " "
Thomas Howe, Valparaiso, "
Michael Harold, " "
James L. Sweeny, Fort Wayne, "
John Fitsgibbons, Lei Gro, "
John Murray, Peru, "
John Sheehy, Lawrenceburgh, "
Owen Cunningham, Chicago, Ills.
W. P. Cardwell, " "
Thomas O'Connor, " "
Charles King, " "
Michael O'Brien, " "
B. P. Heavy, " "
A. L. Morrison, " "
Mortimer Scanlan, " "
Richard O'Malley, " "
Nicholas Crickard, " "
P. McMahon, Amboy, "
Michael Larkin, Rock Island, "
John Mulvany, Gilman, "
Thomas Haire, Quincy, "
Thomas Corcoran, " "
Thomas O'Hare, Galesburg, "
Thomas Traynor. " "
William Rigney, Morris, "
John Ryan, Joliet, "
W. Stapleton, " "
Frank Shields, Wilmington, "
John McManus, " "
John Howley, Cairo, "
Thomas C. Dwyer, " "
M. J. Hennessey, " "
Alexander Vaughey, Seneca, "
John Forristal, La Salle, "
Joseph Hayes. " "
Thomas O'Leary, Alton, "
Dennis Riordan, Springfield, "
A. A. Bushell, Peoria, "
M. H. Enneberry, " "
P. K. Barrett, " "
Francis Doyle, Bloomington, "
Patrick Buckley, Camp Point, "
James Nowlan, Mount Sterling, "

Joseph H. Barry, Galena,	Ills.
John F. Finnerty,	"	"
Cornelius Kelly, Danville,	"
Thomas Hackett, Louisville, Ky.,
Dennis Lincoln,	"	"
James McDermott,	"	"
Patrick Shea,	"	"
John H. Ryan,	"	"
Michael Dawson,	"	"
John A. Geary, Lexington,	"
John Rodgers,	"	"
Thos. McNamara,	"
John L. Kemple, New Orleans, La.,
Thos. McCarthy, Nashville, Tenn.,
Martin Kerrigan,	"	"
J. P. McGrath,	"	"
Daniel Dohey,	"	"
John Kennedy,	"	"
William Moran, St. Louis, Mo.,
Philip Coyne,	"	"
Francis Crump,	"	"
Edward O'Sullivan,	"	"
M. W. Hagan,	"	"
Martin Brennan,	"	"
J. C. Carroll, St. Charles,	"
Daniel Haggerty,	"	"
P. J. Haire, Hannibal,	"
Thomas Fagan,	"	"
T. Neville, Ottumwa, Iowa,
P. Gibbons, Keokuk,	"
Wm. Butler,	"	"
M. O'Donnell, McGregor, Iowa,
J. W. O'Brien,	"	"
R. S. Quinn, Davenport,	"
Patrick Ryder, Lansing,	"
Cornelius Ryan, Elkader,	"
P. P. Freeman, Iowa City,	"
J. C. Burns, Dubuque,	"
John L. Vaughan,	"	"
M. McShane, Burlington,	"
Henry O'Connor, Muscatine,	"
Lawrence Verdon, Detroit, Michigan,
James Holighan,	"	"
Miles J. O'Reilly,	"	"
John Monaghan,	"	"
Richard Whallen, Ontonagan,	"
Stephen O'Brien, Grand Rapids,	"
Bernard Courtney,	"	"

Daniel Meagher, Wyandotte,	Mich.,
Christopher Gohegan, Rockland, "
Jeremiah Quinn, Milwaukie, Wis.,
J. White,	"	"
M. J. Ryan,	"	"
Martin Gavin,	"	"
James Flynne, Fond du Lac,	"
M. Lavelle Prairie du Chien,	"
James Fielding, Racine,	"
Martin C. Gannon, Osh Kosh,	"
H. O'Leary, Greenbay,	"
Daniel T. Scanlan, Janesville, "
John A. Byrne, Madison,	"
Kieran Tierney,	"	"
Michael Ralphe, Winona, Minesota,
A. D. McSweeny, St. Paul,	"
William Jackson, Atchison, Kansas,
J. Quinlan, Leavenworth,	"
Jere'h. Kavanagh, San Francisco, Cal.,
Dennis J. McCarthy,	"	"
John Shields,	"	"
John Henneberry, Sacramento,	"
F. S. McGuire, San Jose,	"
Samuel Fitzsimmons, Sawyer's Bar, "
Patrick Fenton, Santa Clara,	"
E, O'Donnell, Alcatray Island,	"
John O'Garra, Eureka,	"
Hugh A. Kelly, Moore's Flat,	"
T. J. Ahern, Presidio,	"
James Lackey, Washington, D. C.,
T. J. O'Connell,	"	"
*	*	*	Canada,
*	*	*	"
*	*	*	"

Thomas A. Smyth, Brig. Gen.,
	Army of Potomac,
John H. Gleason, Col.,
Mathew Murphy, Col.,	"
James McDonnell, 5th N. H.,	"
Lt. J. McCarthy, Nansemond,	"
Dr. Lawrence Reynolds, "	"
Capt. D. P. Conyngham,
	Army of Tennessee,
Lt. Col., W. G. Halpin,
	Army of Cumberland,
Col B. F. Mullen,	"
Colonel McGroarty,	"

ADDRESS
OF THE
Second Congress
OF THE
FENIAN BROTHERHOOD,
HELD IN THE CITY OF CINCINNATI, OHIO.
• From January 17th to 20th, 1865,
TO THE IRISH OF AMERICA.

FELLOW-COUNTRYMEN —The Chief Officers, Centres and Delegates of the Fenian Brotherhood in the Congress assembled, have resolved to address their fellow-exiles in America, on the subject of their beloved fatherland, so as to direct their attention seriously to the condition of that country past and present, and to urge them to co-operate with their organization in the work of its deliverance.

Though forced by oppression and dire necessity into foreign countries, Ireland is still your faithful heritage: her hills, her valleys, her fields and woods and streams are yours, on the worlds broad surface its your own proper home. You are strangers wherever else you go, and no matter how fortune may favor you, if your hearts are true, upon your lips the bread of exile will prove bitter. You owe to that dear land your first and warmest love. It is the portion of the world decreed in the economy of Providence to be the dwelling place of your race, and deprived of it you are a people without a country. And, vain will be your longing for a return to your native land; vain will be your desire to live again amid the scenes where you were born, and to sleep your last sleep in the graves of your fathers, if you do not in this her hour of direst need give your aid, your means, your labor, your life, if necessary, to break the power of your country's enemies, and to invest her with the noble attributes of genuine independence.

The only organization that has enunciated the true principles of Irish independence, since the days of Wolfe Tone and Emmett, is the Fenian Brotherhood, whose Congress now addresses you. Other associations have risen up from time to time, promising great things for your native country; but they trifled with the people, and reduced them to the condition of Lazarus at the gates of the Dives' of this world. The Fenian Brotherhood will neither fawn nor cringe, nor beg; but rising to the dignity of true manhood, it proposes to send means and men across the sea, and redress Ireland's wrongs where alone they can effectually be redressed, on the field of battle. It is to be prepared for that issue, that we have undertaken to organize the Irish people, believing that such organization is essential to success. If you do not sympathise with the English garrison in Ireland, you will appreciate our motives, and enrol yourself without delay beneath our banner, and thus show the glory of our undertaking.

It is as certain as death, that if a bold, quick effort is not made, in a very few years our race and nationality will cease to exist. We say this after the experience of the last twenty years; within that period four millions of our people have been swept from the face of the Irish soil, some have perished of starvation; some were flung into the depths of the Atlantic; some died in Canada: while the bones of others are bleaching on all the battle-fields of Europe and America, and the remainder are dragging out a miserable existence as "hewers of wood and drawers of water," in every clime beneath the sun.

When Jeremiah contemplated the ruin of Jerusalem, and the deep desolation of his country, he cried out in the bitterness of his soul—"Oh, that my head was water, and my eyes a fountain of tears, that I might weep day and night for the slain of the daughter of my people!" Jeremiah was a patriot as well as a prophet—he loved his country and mourned her fate; but Jerusalem, in the lowest depths of her misery. never presented to the eyes of mankind, or the sympathies of a prophet, the dreadful picture that Ireland presents to the world at this day. Ireland! once known to the nations as the island of saints and sages, of warriors and chiefs, whose sons went forth scattering broadcast, with generous hand, those treasures of science and art, which shone with such resplendent glory amid the darkness of the middle ages, is now known to mankind as the nation of beggars, for whose people (your kindred and ours) the begging box goes round, asking alms from year to year.

This revolting state of things is not the natural condition of Ireland, and is inconsistent with the providence of God. His providence is seen in the luxuriant crops that reward the toil of the industrious peasant; but the hellish will of the Irish landlord is seen in the seizure of these crops for rack-rent, thus reducing their producer to beggary and starvation and death. The Providence of God is seen in the abundant harvests, and in the rich pastures of your native hills and plains; but the will of the foreign spoiler is seen in the desolation of Irish homesteads, where the fire is quenched on the hearth-stone, where the torch has been put to the roof-tree, and the once happy family has been driven out to die upon the soil which is of right their own. Hushed is the voice of the Irish mother in many a home that had ever a "Cead mille failthe" for the stranger, and gave to him the right of hospitality. In many a place that once rung with the cheerful hum of life and industry, silence now reigns unbroken, save by the lowing of horned cattle and the cry of the alien herdsmen. And still the fearful work goes on; still famine stalks abroad; still the emigrant ship unfurls her sails, and bears away to an ocean grave, or to stranger lands the bone and sinew of our race. Soon, very soon, the sun of Irish Nationality will have set forever in sorrow and shame, and the green graves wherein repose the bones of our fathers beneath the old abbeys, blessed by the hand of religion, and watered by kindred tears for generations, will be desecrated by the hoofs of Durham cattle. In a few years but a wretched remnant of the old race will remain to bear testimony of their country's wrongs, unless the men of to-day rise up wherever they are, by the Thames, the Clyde, the St. Lawrence, or the Ganges, in the city, in the town, and the hamlet—in the mines, in the forges, in the factories—on the farms and in the forums—the counting-houses, and the workshops, and resolve that they will band together as brothers, to rescue Ireland from the doom to which her merciless foe has destined her. Is not that Irishman a knave, a coward, and a traitor who will forsake his country in this hour of her greatest peril.

It is our conviction, fellow-countrymen, that England's power must be utterly overthrown in Ireland if our country is ever to be saved. Can this be done? It most assuredly can, if the men of Irish race but do even half their duty. Let those of us that are in exile give arms and trained soldiers to our countrymen at home—rifles of the best description, and competent teachers to instruct them in the manner they should be used. Of these we have a sufficient number in America who served in the armies of the Republic, and who are ready to give their experience and lives if need be. in the service of their country. Give them a few privateers, (we have men enough to man them in our ranks,) launch them fairly on the ocean, with their prows towards the shores of Ireland; as they plough the main. pray to the God of your fathers for their safety and succor, and leave the rest to them. If they triumph, you will be partakers of their glory; if they fall, be it on the battle-field or the scaffold, they will die as their father's died before them, and neither your children nor theirs will ever have to blush for their conduct.

If ever an attempt is to be made to save our perishing country, an organization such as ours is absolutely essential. The Fenian Brotherhood is so constituted that every man who is sincere in his devotion to Ireland, can become a member, without the slightest reference to the class or creed with which he may be connected. Let Fenian circles be established in every community where Irishmen reside, be they large or small, all can aid the work.

Organizers will traverse the different States of the American Union, and we solicit for them a cordial reception from all their countrymen. They will form circles and give all necessary information and explanation to enable those not already working with us to take up the cause and throw their aid and influence into it.

The report of this Congress will show that the entire body has implicit confidence in its chief officers and in the measures devised by them to secure our final success. Circles should rely on their State Centres, and all on the chief executive. You, who are not Fenians, may ask—"Is it not possible that you may find your confidence misplaced or your cause betrayed?" With the man who presides over this great organization we are thoroughly acquainted. The unblemished integrity of his character and the self-sacrificing devotedness which, at home and in exile, in weal and woe, he has ever manifested in the cause of his country, are to us more than sufficient evidence that to no safer keeping could her best interests be possibly entrusted.

We have been assailed in many ways by our enemies, personally, politically and religiously. We have with patient endurance borne and braved it all. Our assailants are silenced. We have no reproach to fling upon them, no disposition to assail them in return. By doing so, we would only prove ourselves unfit for the work we have undertaken. Conscious of the righteousness of our cause, and violating no law, save the invader's law of wrong and robbery, we are determined to advance with unwavering purpose, irrespective of the opinions or accusations of our country's enemies.

Fellow-countrymen, we desire that every man of Irish birth and lineage who loves Ireland and is willing to aid in her restoration, shall become a member of the Fenian Brotherhood. Within ourselves we shall then have the power to free our country, and united, our triumph will be an absolute certainty. Why do you hesitate? We propose to you no new political creed. What we teach is the truth of old, the gospel of righteous revolution, the faith that triumphed at Clontarf and Benburb and at the Pass of Plumes and every place on earth where freedom has been fought for and gloriously won.

In conclusion, fellow-countrymen, we would appeal to you, as you love your native land and desire to see it free, to rally under our banners, and join with us hand to hand and heart to heart, that we may go forward united with the steady tread of soldiers to smite to death the enemies of our country and raise her to a distinguished place of independence among the nations of the earth.

JAMES GIBBONS,
H. O'C. McCARTHY,
P. F. WALSH.

The above address was presented by Mr. James Gibbons, of Philadelphia, Penna. In offering it to the Convention, that gentleman said :—

GENTLEMEN OF THE SECOND IRISH CONGRESS:—On behalf of the Committee, I will say, in submitting this, our report, that we confess our total inability to speak in suitable language on this most important occasion. While doing so, we are fully impressed with the conviction that no created intelligence can portray in colors, dark and damning as they should be, the cruelties perpetrated on our afflicted people by the robber and the murderer in the name of a legal government. Four thousand miles away from our kindred and our home, we cannot escape from British rule; and if in the language of holy writ, we could take the wings of the morning, and fly to the uttermost ends of the earth, the cry of our famine stricken people would find us there, and add to the bitter bread of exile, *wormwood and gall*.

Among the many hellish devices of our enemy, was the passage of a law to prevent you from meeting in convention, in a legislative capacity, so that Ireland's people have had no legislative representation, since the confederation of Killkenny.

'Tis true, a *thing* called an Irish Parliament sat in Dublin, but it then was foreign to the soil, and hostile to the people. Unable to resist the goadings of a guilty conscience, it committed suicide—it perished, and infamy is written on its *tomb*.

ADDRESS
OF THE
IRISH NATIONAL CONGRESS
OF THE
FENIAN BROTHERHOOD,
ASSEMBLED AT CINCINNATI, OHIO, U. S. A.
From January 17th to 20th, 1865,
TO THE PEOPLE OF IRELAND.

COUNTRYMEN AND BROTHERS,—We, the officers and delegates of the Fenian Brotherhood here assembled, represent the many thousands of Irish Nationalists who are united in this great organization, and who reside on different parts of the North American continent with one mind, with one spirit, with one deliberate and determined purpose we have met, and our resolve is that Ireland shall be free.

Not for three hundred years has the Irish race been so largely and so truly represented as it is in this assembly, such is the conviction of those who, from knowledge of our country's history and from interest in her sacred cause, are best qualified to form an impartial judgment. We feel that, under such circumstances, it would neither be consistent with the claims of duty nor with the dictates of affection, for us to separate without addressing a few words of greeting, of counsel and of encouragement to our friends and brothers who are still permitted to remain in the land of our birth.

Although an ocean rolls between us, we clasp in spirit to-day the hands of those who, not only by blood and birth, but in heart and soul and settled purpose, are one with ourselves. With their members and their strength with their enlightened intelligence and admirable spirit, we are thoroughly acquainted, and while we cordially congratulate them on the noble progress which they have already made along the only road by which they can ever recover and re-conquer the lost liberties of our country—we are assured that it will encourage them to advance on their high career to be informed that, on this side of the Atlantic, our members in this great Irish organization have been multiplied at least four-fold during the last fourteen months, and are still rapidly increasing. Our members are to a man true hearted Irishmen of different classes and creeds, but all united as with a single soul in the cause of Ireland, so that at length the time appears to have arrived when division, the ruin and curse of our country, will be driven back discomfited to the hell from which our enemies worked it ; and, although it is still unfortunately true that our foes continue to "join in hate." we, on the other hand, have been taught by sad experience the duty and necessity of "joining in love." It thus becomes morally certain that when the hour for action comes, our countrymen of every shade of opinion will be only anxious to forget their petty differences, and to unite for their country's liberty. The question then will be not between one class of Irishmen and another, but between united Ireland and her hereditary enemy.

It is, perhaps, not unnatural for our brothers at home to enquire why it is that, with such numbers and resources as ought to be available on this American continent for the salvation of Ireland, the great object of our organic existence is still unaccomplished? Our reply is easy. It is simply to point to the enormous difficulties with which we have to contend, and which it is only of late we have begun effectually to conquer. Escaping from worse than Egyptian bondage, with little more than their lives, our unhappy countrymen have to fight hard for existence, when flung upon a foreign shore. This so engrosses their energies that the cause of their country too often sinks into obeyance. The dreadful dishonesty of too many of those who, since the era of the accursed Union, have taken a prominent part in Irish politics, and the disastrous failure of almost every movement in which the national Irish heart was interested, have gone far to deprive the Irish people of all faith even in men whose honesty of purpose the breath of slander can never tarnish, or in measures which once they are supported with the hands, as well as by the hearts and voices, of the millions of our race are more than adequate not only to free Ireland but to scatter her enemies like chaff before the storm. And, in addition to all this, the foul farce of parliamentary agitation in Ireland being utterly exploded and execrated, you, our brothers at home, betook yourselves as duty bound you to do to the only available resource left to you, and that was to devote yourselves to that *cool and quiet and persistent preparation*, which alone can enable you to perform successfully the great work that lies before you. But, you will observe, that this placed your friends in other lands, and especially in free America, in a somewhat peculiar position. They were no longer able to point to "monster meetings." which, although most likely empty of all good, are calculated to impress and impose on the ignorant and unreflecting. And being resolved, as you are, not to exchange masters, but to free your country from foreign oppression, and to restore its soil to its rightful proprietors—the people—you who have, as a matter of course, no array of aristocratic names which have hitherto been generally employed to dazzle and blind the eyes of dupes, whose country these aristocrats have ever been ready to betray, and on whose labor they are accustomed to live. With these and other obstacles, this organization had long and wearily to contend. It has conquered them all. It is now one of the great facts of the age, an undeniable power on the earth—a power whose resolve is firm as the foundations of the everlasting hills, and that resolve is to emancipate Ireland. And it will do it.

Do you ask us when? A public answer to that question would enlighten our foes. But one thing is certain, the day of deliverance comes on apace. It may be, and probably is, very near; your duty and ours is to improve every hour, and strain every energy, that we may be ready for it when it arrives.

The work, brothers and friends, must be done mainly if not exclusively by ourselves. No men ever had an independent country who did not fight for it. No men who refuse to do so are worthy of such a boon. No men ever will preserve the independence of their country who are not ready at all times to devote labor and limb and life to its defence. This is the lesson of universal experience. Gainsay it who will; its truth is as manifest as the light of the noonday summer's sun. We are resolved to aid you in every way by whatever resources may be in our power. But to you, Irishmen in Ireland, the cause of our country is and must be mainly entrusted, whether it be to destroy its enemies, or to guard its liberties. To the first part of this grand and glorious duty, your attention should, above all other things, be perpetually directed. Political adventurers who, like their predecessors, are resolved to sell the country for pay and place and power, will invite you to join with them in constitutional agitations and petitions to the parliament of your enemies and oppressors. You will be asked to vote for pseudo-patriots, and to send them to the Saxon capital to prove themselves traitors to Ireland by sitting in the legislature of England. Treat all such movements with contempt, and by every proper means discourage and suppress them.

Remain for the present at your posts in Ireland. If you can possibly help it, let nothing induce you to forsake your country. The fate of the emigrant is seldom an enviable one. And we who address you know by bitter experience that the instances are few in which men and women of Irish birth ever find themselves at home or happy in a foreign land. It is unnecessary to do more than to remind you of the poverty, the misery, and too frequently the crime, with which very many of the Irish people sink after their arrival in America. If the morality and integrity, not to speak of more sacred hings, are to be preserved, it can only be effectually done by retaing them in the land of where they were born.

Had we, fellow-countrymen, abandoned the proud hope of Ireland being ever free, we would not be the men to council you to remain the degraded serfs of England; but being confident or our native land's approaching deliverance we implore of her children at home to turn their thoughts to something better and more noble than emigration to this or any other country—there is an additional reason and important one, why you should cling to the last to the grand old land, which God has given you for a heritage, and that is that Ireland's resurrection depends in no small degree on the number of Irish hands as shall be ready to strike for it and to maintain it. Therefore we urge you to stand steadfastly where duty to your country and yourselves demands—and that is, with your feet upon your native soil; and as brothers and as men of truth, we promise you that the day is not far distant when we shall stand side by side together on Ireland's sacred shore, a united and embattled host, with the flag of our country floating free above us, and with the power in our hands to tear sceptre and crown from the invader and usurper, and place them in the hand and upon the brow of the beautiful land of our birth.

> JOHN POPE HODNETT, New Jersey.
> A. L. MORRISON, Chicago, Ill.
> J. F. FINNERTY, Chicago, Ill.

[APPENDIX.]

RESOLUTIONS

UNANIMOUSLY PASSED AT THE

First General Congress of the Fenian Brotherhood,

ASSEMBLED IN THE CITY OF CHICAGO AND STATE OF ILLINOIS, ON THE 3RD, 4TH AND 5TH OF NOVEMBER, 1863.

I.

WHEREAS, The time has come when the members of the Fenian Brotherhood feel called upon to declare to the public the nature and object of their organization and their individual rights as freemen and citizens; be it.

Resolved, That we, the Centres and Delegates of the said Fenian Brotherhood, assembled in this our first annual convention, do hereby emphatically proclaim our organization to consist of an association having for its object the national freedom of Ireland, and composed for the most part of Citizens of the United States of America, of Irish birth or descent, but open to such other dwellers on the American continent as are friendly to the liberation of Ireland from the domination of England, by every honorable means within our reach, collectively and individually, save and except such means as may be in violation of the constitution and laws under which we live and to which all of us, who are citizens of the United States, owe our allegiance. We furthermore boldly and firmly assert our unquestionable right under the said constitution and laws to associate together for the above named object, or for any similar one; and to assist with our money, our moral and political influence, or, if it so pleases ourselves, with our persons and our lives in liberating any enslaved land under the sun.

II.

WHEREAS, The exiles of every country, and especially of Ireland, have ever found a home, personal freedom, and equal political rights, in this American Republic; and

WHEREAS, We deem its preservation and success of supreme importance, not alone to ourselves and our fellow-citizens, but to the extension of democratic institutions, and to the well being and social elevation of the whole human race; be it

Resolved, THAT WE, THE REPRESENTATIVES OF THE FENIAN BROTHERHOOD IN THE UNITED STATES, DO HEREBY SOLEMNLY DECLARE, WITHOUT LIMIT OR RESERVATION, OUR ENTIRE ALLEGIANCE, TO THE CONSTITUTION AND LAWS OF THE UNITED STATES OF AMERICA.

III.

WHEREAS, From the hostile attitude assumed by the English oligarchy, merchants, and press towards the United States, since the commencement of the disastrous civil strife that has devastated this Republic during the past three years, it is all but certain that war is imminent, or at least fast approaching, between our adopted country and England, our hereditary enemy; be it

Resolved, That the younger members of the several Circles of the Fenian Brotherhood be instructed to apply themselves sedulously to the study of military tactics and the use of arms, and to organize themselves into companies for the purpose of drilling, so as to be prepared to offer their services to the United States government, by land or sea, against England's myrmidons in that event.

IV.

WHEREAS, We deem the resurrection of Ireland to independent nationhood to be of immediate interest not alone to Irishmen but to all sincere lovers of human freedom, as well as of especial advantage to America, whose vanguard she stands even to-day against British aggression, with her organized sons keeping watch and ward for the United States at the thresholds of the despots of Europe, nay in their very citadels; be it

Resolved, That every man of Irish birth or descent who lives on the American continent is admissible to the Fenian Brotherhood without distinction of class or creed, provided his character be unblemished and his devotion to Ireland unquestioned; and that we earnestly invite every American who is loyal to the principles of self-government to aid and sustain us by his moral influence against our enemies, the emissaries of foreign despotisms, who would feign crush the growth of republican principles and stop the onward march of Freedom by assailing it even in this free land.

V.

WHEREAS, Certain questions connected with the general politics of the United States, with local partizanship foreign to Irish freedom, or with differences in religious faith, are the great obstacles that impede the successful working of the Fenian Brotherhood, and delay the redemption of Ireland, by perpetuating in this country, the ancient dissentions of her sons, though upon issues for the most part peculiar to America; be it

Resolved, That every subject relating to the internal politics of America and the quarrels of American partizans, together with all subjects relating to differences in religion, be absolutely and forever excluded from the councils and deliberations of the Fenian Rrotherhood, and be declared totally foreign to its objects and designs; and that we furthermore invite every sincere friend of liberty, without distinction of party or creed, to join cordially and harmoniously with us upon the neutral platform of Irish Independence.

THE FENIAN BROTHERHOOD NOT A "SECRET," "OATH-BOUND" OR "ILLEGAL" SOCIETY.

VI.

WHEREAS, Certain men, actuated by feelings of hostility, either to the national resurrection and independence of Ireland in particular, or by a general indiscriminate hatred to the principles of self-government and popular sovereignty—to the Republican Idea itself—have repeatedly attacked the Fenian Brotherhood upon false pretences and unfounded assumptions; some asserting that it is a "Secret Society," bound together by an OATH, and, as such, distinctly condemned by the Catholic Church, through certain rescripts thereof, leveled against the Freemasons, Carbonari, Odd Fellows and other similar associations, social or political ; while other assailants confine their attacks to vaguely charging the said brotherhood with being an "Illegal" society and consequently sinful, and without defining the points wherein its illegality consists, and without stating what particular laws have been transgressed, and in what country these laws have been enacted and received,—in a word, whether they be monarchial laws or republican laws, whether we are to look for them in the statute books of the United States or among the ukases of old despotisms of Europe; and

WHEREAS, These accusations having impeded the progress of the cause of the Freedom of Ireland on this continent, we feel called upon to repudiate and deny their truth: be it in the first place

Resolved, That we the members of this convention, most distinctly declare and make known to all whom it may concern, but without the slightest disrespect to any of the societies above-named, that the Fenian Brotherhood is not a Secret Society, inasmuch as no pledge of secresy, expressed or implied, is demanded from the candidates for membership thereof; neither is it an Oath-bound Society, for no oath whatever is required in order to entitle a man to all the privileges of the association. Hence, if the mere fact of its members pledging themselves to secresy can render an association sinful according to the laws of the Catholic Church, there being no pledge of secresy, there can be no sin in becoming a Fenian brother; again, if the mere fact of its members being required to take an oath upon entering it can render it sinful, where there is no oath required there can be no sin, on the grounds above stated, in joining the Fenian Brotherhood.

In the second place be it

Resolved, That we protest most emphatically against the casuistry of the charge made against us of Illegality, inasmuch as the members of the Fenian Brotherhood contemplate no breach of the laws of the United States, while aiding in the liberation of Ireland; and that we challenge our assailants to point out any one instance, wherein our association has transgressed one single provision of the said laws during the past six years, for so long has it existed, and, if it has, let it be indicted by the legal officers of the American Government, and let the question be decided in the American Courts of Justice, for these are the only arbiters that we acknowledge upon questions involving Illegality ; that we nevertheless fully admit that our association may possibly be open to the charge of being illegal, if tested by the laws of England, but these we have repudiated on taking the oath of allegiance to the United States, an act which we know to be illegal, according to the latter code, but not on that account the less right and just.

In the third place be it

Resolved, That, while we conduct ourselves as law-abiding citizens of these United States, we most firmly and emphatically protest against, repudiate and resist all interference with the legitimate exercise of our civic and social priviledge as Freemen under the American constitution on the part of any man or class of men, AND MORE ESPECIALLY ON THE PART OF THOSE WHO MAY CLAIM TO REPRESENT OR TO RECEIVE INSTRUCTIONS FROM ANY FOREIGN POTENTATE OR FOREIGN OFFICIAL WHATSOEVER ; for, were we to submit to such interference, we would be unworthy of participating in the great political privileges, wherewith the naturalized citizens of America are invested.

GENERAL FORM OF FENIAN PLEDGE.

VII.

WHEREAS, Certain Circles of the Fenian organization, as well as individual members thereof, have, in a few instances, adopted forms of pledges peculiar to themselves; and

WHEREAS, These forms, by falling into the hands of our enemies, have subjected. the said organization to misrepresentation and calumny; and, while we do not forbid any member to take any form of pledge that may please himself with respect either to the redemption of Ireland or to any other subject, provided the same be not hostile to our cause,—be it

Resolved, In order to prevent misconception as to our obligations in future, that the following be adopted as the only form that shall henceforth be obligatory, in order to entitle a candidate to all the rights and privileges of membership in the Fenian Brotherhood:—

"I ———— solemnly pledge my sacred word of honor as a truthful and honest man, that I will labor with earnest zeal for the liberation of Ireland from the yoke of England, and for the establishment of a free and independent government on Irish soil; that I ———— will implicitly obey the commands of my superior officers in the Fenian Brotherhood; that I will faithfully discharge the duties of my membership, as laid down in the Constitution and By-Laws thereof; that I will do my utmost to promote feelings of love, harmony, and kindly forbearance among all Irishmen; and that I will foster, defend and propagate the aforesaid Fenian Brotherhood to the utmost of my power."

PERVADING SENTIMENTS AND PRESENT POSITION OF THE IRISH RACE ABROAD AND AT HOME.

VIII.

WHEREAS, It is a self-evident and incontrovertible fact, that a profound love of Ireland, and a never-ceasing longing for her liberation from foreign domination are all but universal throughout the whole Irish Race, at home and abroad; and,

WHEREAS, It is equally manifest that the said Irish Race is everywhere pervaded by an intense and undying hatred towards the monarchy and oligarchy of Great Britain, which have so long ground their country to the dust, hanging her patriots, starving out her people, and sweeping myriads of Irish men, women, and children off their paternal fields, to find a refuge in foreign lands, bringing with them thither a burning desire for the destruction of British tyranny, and bequeathing this feeling as an heir-loom to their posterity; be it

Resolved. That it is the special duty of the members of the Fenian Brotherhood to strive with all their might, and with their whole heart, to create and foster amongst Irishmen everywhere, feelings of fraternal harmony and kindly love of each other, unity of counsel, and a common policy upon the Irish question, with mutual forbearance upon all others, so that their efforts may be unanimously directed towards the common object of their universal wishes after a common preconcerted plan. Thus will their force become irresistible, guided by one will and one purpose, in one undeviating system of action, and thus will they give shape and life, direction and movement to that love of Ireland, and that hatred of her oppressors, which are the predominant passions of every true Irish heart.

IX.

WHEREAS, The men of Irish birth and lineage, now dwelling on the American continent, hold at present, a more powerful position among the peoples of the earth, in point of numbers, political privileges, social influence and military strength than was ever before held by any exiled portion, not alone of the Irish nation, but of any subjugated nation whatsoever; and,

WHEREAS, We feel firmly convinced that her British tyrants could not keep Ireland much longer enthralled, if the Irish citizens of the American Republic were closely allied to and cordially co-operating for the redemption of their fatherland, with their brethren still living on the Irish soil, together with those expatriated Irishmen, who are planted by thousands, *like so many hostile garrisons throughout Great Britain, in the very centres of her manufacturing and commercial wealth, throughout her colonies, and even in her imperial capital, driven from their ancestral homes by the fell agencies of the tyrannical laws of England;* be it

Resolved, That we, the representatives of the Fenian Brotherhood labor with all our energies and talents, with stern will, steadfast zeal, and ceaseless exertion, to organize, combine and concentrate these great elements of Irish national power, which an all-wise Providence has. it would seem, FOR THE PURPOSES OF RETRIBUTIVE JUSTICE, placed within the reach of the present generation of Irishmen; and that we direct their whole force, moral and material, from all points towards the overthrow of British tyranny in Ireland, and the establishment of an independent government in its stead.

X.

WHEREAS, We feel confident that the numbers and importance of the Irish element in the United States, England and her colonies, as well as the Irish power scattered elsewhere over the earth, on land and sea, have at this particular epoch, reached their greatest developement, and that henceforth, they must rapidly, decrease by the natural decay of humanity, inasmuch as Ireland, the source of their production, with her diminished population, is no longer able to fill up their places, as they die out—to supply the "wear and tear" to which they are subjected in the hard battle of the exile's life; and,

WHEREAS, This declension of the Irish people abroad, must be accompanied by the almost total extinction of the Irish race at home; if it be not speedily prevented by the destruction of the power which is causing it; and,

WHEREAS, Also, the thousands of well trained Irish American soldiers and the officers, who are at present, longing to strike for the freedom of their fatherland, will dwindle away in equal ratio, if no opportunity be given them to serve their own country, while the vigor of their manhood remains unbroken. be it

Resolved, That we call upon and exhort every true Irishman in America, England and the British Colonies, to rally around the Fenian Brotherhood, and to aid us 'in preparing Ireland for freedom's battle, and in hastening the day of her deliverance; and that we, with equal fervor exhort our brothers in Ireland to hold by our beloved land to the last extremity, nor flee from it to foreign countries; to gird their loins silently and sternly, for the inevitable struggle that is approaching, and TO AVOID ALL PUBLIC MEETINGS AND ELECTIONEERING DELUSIONS, which only serve to expose good men to the persecution of village despots, and which are as bloodhounds to track out the best and most devoted of the Irish race, and start them up to be hunted and exterminated like wild beasts by their oppressors.

IRISH NATIONALITY INDESTRUCTIBILITY.—RIGHT TO INDEPENDENCE.

XI.

WHEREAS, Ever since the first invasion of their country by Henry the Second of England and his Norman freebooters the people of Ireland have, from generation to generation, given undeniable evidence of their INDESTRUCTIBILITY, by periodical resistance to their foreign tyrants, ever protesting against the extinction of their independence, by the blood of illustrious martyrs, shed both on the battle-field and on the scaffold; be it

Resolved, THAT WE DECLARE THE SAID IRISH PEOPLE TO CONSTITUTE ONE OF THE DISTINCT NATIONALITIES OF THE EARTH, AND AS SUCH JUSTLY ENTITLED TO ALL THE RIGHTS OF SELF-GOVERNMENT.

THE I. R. D.—THE C. E.

† XII.

WHEREAS.   *   *   *   *   *   *   *

*   *   *   *   *   *   *   *   *   *   *

*   *   *   *   * be it

Resolved, That   *   *   *   *   *   *   *

*   *   *   *   *   *   *   *   *   *   *

*   *   *   *   *   *   *   *   *   *   *

*   *   *   *   *

XIII.

WHEREAS,   *   *   *   *   *   *   *

*   *   *   * be it

Resolved, That   *   *   *   *   *   *   *

*   *   *   *   *   *   *   *   *

XIV.

WHEREAS,   *   *   *   *   *   *   *   *   *   *

*   *   *   *   be it

Resolved, That   *   *   *   *   *   *

*   *   *   *   *   *   *   *   *   *   *

---

† *The twelfth, thirteenth and fourteenth series of preambles and resolutions are withheld at present from the public, their publication at this time being deemed injudicious.*

SYMPATHY WITH POLES.

XV.

WHEREAS, The precedent set to Irishmen by the noble and almost desperate struggle, which the gallant sons and faithful daughters of Poland are at present maintaining against the giant despotism of Russia, their country's foe, fills our hearts at once with an enthusiastic admiration of their brave and patriotic devotion, with a sincere love for their holy cause, and with a heartfelt respect for their sufferings in its behalf, as well as with a generous emulation to follow their great example; and,

WHEREAS, When we compare our own position with theirs—our own numerous vantage grounds for acting against our foe and our incalculable superiority in external resources, which the tyrants of Ireland cannot reach, with the isolated position of the Poles, hemmed in all round by enemies, and with so few of their people beyond the grasp of their tyrants.—our frivolous dissensions with their glorious and fraternal concord,—we are struck with shame and humiliation by the contrast presented to us; therefore, be it

Resolved, That we express our deep and heartfelt sympathy with the People of Poland in their war against their oppressors; our admiration of their indomitable fortitude. and the grandeur of their present attitude before mankind, and our ardent prayers that their efforts may be crowned with complete success.

And be it further

Resolved, That we hereby express our reverential gratitude and filial respect towards his Holiness, Pope Pius the Ninth, for his paternal solicitude in the cause of suffering Poland, up in arms for her liberty. and for the anxious care with which he offers up to Heaven his ardent aspirations for her success, and recommends her brave sons, battling for "right against might," to the prayers and the support of the Catholic world.

PERSEVERANCE—FORM OF ORGANIZATION.

XVI.

WHEREAS, We are fully impressed with the magnitude of the task undertaken by the Fenian Brotherhood, and well aware of the difficulties and delays that may retard its accomplishment, but are nevertheless resolved to persevere steadfastly and with active zeal in our efforts until they shall be crowned with complete success, in the firm and implicit faith that

> "THE PATIENT DINT AND POWDER SHOCK
> CAN BLAST AN EMPIRE LIKE A ROCK."

Therefore be it

Resolved, That the Fenian Brotherhood, be declared hereby A FIXED AND PERMANENT INSTITUTION in America, and that it continue its labors without ceasing until Ireland shall be restored to her rightful place among free nations.

XVII.

WHEREAS, The members of the Fenian Brotherhood are for the most part citizens of a free and democratic republic, and hence entitled to a system of government and direction in accordance with the institutions and customs of America; be it

Resolved, That a general convention of representatives of its several branches shall be held at such stated time and place as shall be hereafter determined on for the purposes of receiving reports of its progress and expenditure, approving or condemning the conduct and management of its executive corps, and of devising such rules and regulations as may become necessary for its droper government by the requirements of the future; and that the said convention shall be composed of the Head Centre, the State Centres, and the Centres of Circles, assisted by Elected Delegates from all circles in good standing, each circle being entitled to elect one delegate, but no more.

And be it moreover

Resolved, That a Head Centre be elected at the said general convention with power to govern and direct the affairs of the whole organization during the ensuing year, and that a Central Treasurer and Assistant Central Treasurer and Central Council consisting of Five Members, be elected for a like period on the same occasion, for the purpose of assisting the Head Centre in the discharge of his duties by their advice and support.

XVIII

WHEREAS, In the peculiar position of the Fenian Brotherhood, placed almost in presence of a powerful and ever vigilant enemy, it is absolutely necessary for the prompt execution and ultimate success of its efforts that its chief officer should be invested with ample executive powers; be it

Resolved, That the Head Centre be entrusted with the whole management of the affairs of said Brotherhood, during his term of office, subject, however, to the control of the Central Council, should he outstrip the limits prescribed to him by its Constitution and By-Laws, as agreed upon at this Convention, and to such restrictions as may hereafter be imposed upon him at any future general Convention, regularly called together; that the said Head Centre shall have the power to confirm or annul the election of all State Centres and Centres of Circles; that it shall be his prerogative to treat on the part of the said Fenian Brotherhood with all parties that are likely to favor or assist in the redemption of Ireland and in the downfall of English tyranny; whether those parties be regularly established governments, bodies corporate, organized societies, public functionaries or private individuals, at home or abroad; that through the said Head Centre alone shall the Brotherhood receive any communication from any party whatsoever, and that he alone is entitled to enter into engagements with them in our behalf.

XIX.

WHEREAS, Occasions of sudden emergency may arise when the representatives of the Brotherhood may have to be called together in Convention, either by State Organizations or in General Assembly; be it

Resolved, That the Head Centre shall be empowered to call a special Convention, either of the whole Brotherhood or of the State Organizations thereof, with the consent of the Central Council or without it, on receiving a written requisition therefor from ten Centres of Circles established within the limits of the district to be represented at the said Convention.

XX.

WHEREAS, It is requisite for the purpose of facilitating the transaction of business by equal izing the labor of conducting so widely extended an organization as the Fenian Brotherhood, that there should be a regular gradation of divisions and sub-divisions thereof, and that under the Head Centre there should be a regular gradation of officers to preside over them; be it

Resolvved, That the said Brotherhood be divided into State Organizations, Circles, and Sub-Circles, and that they be presided over and governed respectively by State Centres, Centres and Sub-Centres.

XXI.

Finally, and in commemoration of our cordial and sincere participation in the acts and resolutions of this, our first general Convention; be it

Resolved, That we, the representatives of the Fenian Brotherhood here assembled, do solemly pledge ourselves, without mental reservation, to abide by the foregoing resolutions in spirit and in truth, and that we will faithfully abide by the Constitution and By-Laws, as passed by us for the government and guidance of our organization, and that we also pledge ourselves to extend foster and sustain the said brotherhood to the utmost of our ability, and that in testimony thereof we hereunto affix our signatures.

James Gibbons, Philadelphia, Pa. Michael Scanlan, Chicago, Ill. P. F. Walsh, late Captain 84th Pa. Vols., Pittsburg, Pa. Michael Cavill Philadelphia. P. T. Sherlock, 23d Illinois Vols. James M. Fitzgerald, Captain 10th Ohio. John O'Carroll, Broad Top, Pa. Daniel Grady, Washington, D. C.

Daniel Donovau, Lawrence, Mass. J. J. Fitzgibbon, Chicago, Ill. Henry O'C. McCarthy Chicago, Ill. John Stauton, Troy, N. Y. Thomas Nash, Indianapolis, Ind. John A. Stuart, Indianapolis, Ind. Robert Kennington, Indianapolis, Ind. Thomas Redmond, Indianapolis, Ind. T. Constantine, Bowling Green, Ky. John Cosgrove, New Albany, Ind. Thomas McCarthy, Nashville Tenn. J. P. McGrath, Louisville, Ky. James Manning, Cleveland, Ohio. Andrew Fagan, Cleveland, Ohio. Patrick Gorman. Logansport, Ind. John Carroll, Crawfordsville, Ind. Patrick O'Farrell, Covington, Ind. James S. McMahen, Covington, Ind. Michael Fitzpatrick, Lafayette, Ind. Robert Sheeley, Lafayette, Ind. Matthew Ball, Lafayette, Ind. Richard O'Meara, Lafayette, Ind. Patrick Murray, Lafayette, Ind. John Cunningham. Lafayettee, Bnd. T. F. Kelly, Springfield, Ill. D. O. Crowly, Springfield, Ill, Michael Gleason, Springfield, Ill. John Cavanagh, Springfield, Ill. P. H. McLear, Springfield, Ill. Titus Scullen, Danville, Ill. E. Osborne, Terra Haute, Ind. C. H. O'Brien, Terra Haute, Ind. P. Byrne, Madison, John Mullany, Columbus, Ind. Thomas Dolan, Upper Sandusky, Ohio. John Moran, Sandusky, Ohio. Patrick J. Downing, Major 42d N. Y. Vol. Potomac Circle. D. J. Downing, Capt. 97th N. Y., Potomac Circle. Thomas Hare, Quincy, Ill Thomas O'Mara, Quincy, Ill. D. P. Carmody. Milwaukie, Wis. Bartholomew O'Neil, Milwaukie, Wis. Jeremiah Quinn, Milwaukie, Wis. P. F. Hannan, Major of Phœnix Brigade, New York City. P. O'Rourke, N. Y. A. A. Bushnell, Peoria, Ill. P. W. Dunn, Peoria, Ill. John O'Donnell, Mitchell, Ind. John Gorman, Syracuse, N. Y. William Moran, St. Louis, Mo. William Kidney, St. Louis, Mo. Andrew Wynne, Philadelphia, Pa. T. R. Bourke, Captain 9th Mass. Vol., Circle of Rappahannock. Patrick O'Neil, Circle U. S. Engineers. Matthew Murphy, Col. 69th N. Y. V., N. G. A., Circle of Nansemond. * * * British Provinces. Daniel Quirk, Capt. 23d Ill. V., Terrence O'Mahony, Columbus, Ohio. Thomas Holt, Waterford, N. Y. James Lackey, Washington, D. C. Michael Corcoran, Brig. Gen. Michael J. Heffernan, 14th U. S. Infantry, late of Tipperary, Ireland. William Sullivan, Tiffin, Ohio. Richard Doherty, Lafayette, Ind. James W. Fitzgerald, Cincinnati, Ohio. Patrick Graham, Pittsburgh, Pa. Jeremiah Cavanagh, San Francisco, Cal. John P. Duffiey, Major 35th Ind. * * * Canada East. John O'Brien, Buffalo, N. Y. J. Warren, Boston, Mass. William Meagher, West Troy, N. Y. John O'Mahony, New York. Patrick Leonard, Lieut. Col. Phœnix Brigade, N. Y. John Murphy, Hamilton Rowan Club, N. Y. Francis Welpley, 60th N. Y. V. N. A., Corcoran Legion. M. O'K. Austen, State Line, Ind. William Griffin, Madison, Indiana. Francis Duffy, Lafayette, Ind. James McDermott, Louisville, Kentucky. Peter McFarland, Leavenworth, Kansas. Joseph Kearney, Logansport, Ind. James Carroll, Attica, Ind. James McNamara, Toledo, Ohio. William Hayes, West Point Ind.